I0737843

FROM ARRAH WANNA TO MULE SHOE

MISFIT STORIES FROM MISSPENT LIVES

KELLEY BAKER + MARK A. NOBLES

Copyright

Copyright © 2019 by Kelley Baker & Mark A. Nobles

First Printing, 2019

Abdullah the Butcher originally appeared in Cowboy Jamboree, 2019
The Red Moon originally appeared in Cleaver Magazine, 2019
Eastern Shore originally appeared in Panther City Review, 2016
Pot Roast from Vance Godbey's originally
appeared in Cowboy Jamboree, 2019
Slipstreams originally appeared in Panther City Review, 2018
The Cat Had Been Calico originally appeared in Exhuming Alexandria, 2018
Twas The Night Before The Night Before Christmas
originally appeared in Buckman Journal 2019

BOOK DEDICATION

To my Parents who influenced my past
My Daughter who influences my present
And my future Grand Child who influences my future
-- Kelley Baker

There are three kinds of men.
The one that learns by reading.
The few who learn by observation.
The rest of them have to pee on the electric fence for themselves.
--Will Rogers--

We are what we pretend to be, so we must be
careful about what we pretend to be.
--Kurt Vonnegut--

INTRODUCTION

I first met Mark in 2009 when I was touring Texas promoting my films. He invited me to Fort Worth to do a workshop at a film festival he was organizing. Mark put up my dog Moses and I at his home because Moses was too big for any of the local hotels to feel comfortable with us staying there. Mark had two old rescue dogs and they were great hosts.

We came home late from our first day at the festival and Moses had passed away in Marks living room while we were gone. He was old but it was still a shock. Right away Mark got on the phone and found a place we could take his body, at 10 pm on a Saturday night. It was 40 minutes away. It was well after midnight when we got back to the house. Mark handed me a beer and told me to go sit on the front porch while he cleaned up the living room.

How can I not like this guy?

We've both been writing short stories for years but it wasn't until my visit to Fort Worth on my 2017 book tour that we decided to collaborate on a book of short stories. I was certainly surprised at the similarities of the stories and characters as we never discussed a theme or content. We just put together the stories we liked.

Although I've spent a lot of time all over Texas these last fifteen years, Mark's stories introduced me to Texas and it's people in a different light. I was surprised how much they had in common with the people that populate my stories from the Pacific Northwest. The only real difference seems to be the weather.

The writer and political activist Kay Boyle once said some of her short stories and novels were "Dramatically Autobiographical". I guess the same can be said for some of my stories but you need to remember the word "Dramatically." I always seem to start with an incident or person from my past and then I take the appropriate liberties to compile a good story. If you look hard enough you might be able to figure out what's true, and what isn't.

Hopefully you won't look too hard. You'll just sit back and enjoy all these stories.

--Kelley Baker

I'm an only child. I like my space and privacy. I was in my first year working with a local film festival when I was told by the Executive Director of the festival our keynote talent, who traveled with a behemoth of a dog, had been denied lodgings at the hotel because of the size of said dog. The ED wanted me to house the speaker and his traveling companion in my home. To be honest, I knew nothing about this guy except they called him the 'Angry Filmmaker.'

Suffice to say I was leery of the coming weekend.

Then Kelley and the dog, Moses pulled into my driveway, lumbered out of their van, up my walk, onto my porch, and as it turned out, into my life.

Kelley has already told you Moses passed that weekend. I don't have a lot to add except it was an awkward and uncomfortable situation. What do you say to or do for a man who is on his knees in the middle of your living room floor holding his deceased dog in his arms? I felt I should leave. Give the man some privacy to grieve. But it was late, and it was my house. I had nowhere to go.

The festival was a success. Kelley rocked the house closing night and headed down the road early Monday morning to the next stop on his tour. That should have been the end of the story. But it wasn't. We stayed in touch. We became friends. Over the years on several occasions one or the other of us has remarked how it is odd that we seem to be living different, yet parallel lives. This different, yet parallel aspect is reflected in this collection of misfit stories.

Decide for yourself if you find a shared sensibility of outlook and tone in these stories. Maybe you will, maybe you won't.

Don't believe anything I say. I get paid to make things up.

--Mark A. Nobles

CONTENTS

MARE ISLAND
By Mark A. Nobles

I had just been knocked out of four square and had gone to the back of the line to wait my turn to rejoin the game when Billy Crutchfeld ran up behind me, grabbed my right arm at the elbow and pulled me away. "Hey!" I shouted. I was perturbed because there was easily fifteen minutes still left in recess, and only three people ahead in line, leaving plenty of time to get back in the game.

"Mark, Mark, Mark, MarkMarkMarkMark." Billy liked to say my name repeatedly because he thought it sounded like he was barking like a dog. It was amusing the first half a dozen times, but after that Billy was the only one who continued to giggle.

"I got to talk to you, man, in private," Billy said. Ricky, Jim and Slater ran up behind Billy and formed a semicircle around us. I wondered just how private this conversation needed to be.

"You won't believe it, man," exclaimed Billy.

"You absolutely won't believe it," repeated Jim.

"No way, man," chimed in Slater. Ricky, more out of breath than the others, simply nodded in agreement.

"Beth told Becky to tell me to tell you that Beth likes you!" Billy stood there looking at me with an ear to ear grin.

"Wow!" Jim said, as if hearing the news for the first time.

It seemed to me we all stood there for an eternity. Billy, Jim, Slater and Ricky wearing big ol' grins and eyes as wide as owls, waiting for my reaction.

I stood there, frozen. Frozen motionless and frozen cold. It seemed all life's warmth had drained down my body and out through the soles of my feet. A girl liked me. And not just any girl, Beth O'Riley liked me.

Beth O'Riley was at least the fourth coolest girl in school, maybe as high as third and she was only in the fourth grade. The only two, maybe three, girls cooler than Beth were both sixth graders. A fourth grader being as cool as the coolest sixth graders was unheard of, and actually, had probably never happened in the history of elementary school cool rankings. Anywhere at any time.

I smelled a rat. These boys were yanking my chain. They were way too eager. "No way," I said and began to turn to walk back to the four square line.

"Way!" Billy, Slater, Jim and Ricky all shouted in unison.

"I can prove it," Billy said. He held out his hand to show a perfectly folded piece of paper. It had my name on it, in girly, perfect cursive handwriting. Presumably that was Beth O'Riley's cursive handwriting.

I got really cold again. I was going to catch my death as my ma-maw would say.

"Beth also gave Becky this note for her to give to me to give to you." Billy spoke with the somber tone of a president giving nuclear launch codes.

"Uh uh," I muttered.

"Uh huh," came Billy's retort.

Then we all stared at the note in Billy's hand. He shook it, beckoning me to take it. I reached out and took the note, "Don't shake, don't shake," I told my hand. I gave the note a cursory going over and promptly stuck it in my left front pocket.

"Hey, ain't you going to read it?" asked Ricky.

"I'll read it later," I said as I walked back to the four square line. All four boys looked crestfallen.

"What should I tell Becky?" asked Billy.

"I dunno," I called back. "Tell her you gave me the note, I guess." It was hard to walk. My knees felt like strawberry jelly that had been sitting in the sun. I was thankful that the line had grown to four people. I was even more relieved when the bell rang to call us back to class with one person still ahead of me.

There is absolutely no privacy in elementary school and I needed privacy to read Beth's note. Everyone ran to get in their class line to be marched back into school. I lagged behind everyone partially because my knees were still wobbly and partially because I wanted to be double darn sure Beth got in line well ahead of me. I would have died if our eyes had even skimmed. I stood, last in line, for Mrs. Bailey's class. As she walked by taking the head count, I asked if I could use the restroom.

"Mark, you know the rule. We were just at lunch and recess. You had plenty of time for the restroom before class. Learning is important," she said. Things were always important to Mrs. Bailey. She always started or ended her sentences by telling us how important whatever it was she was talking about.

"I know, Mrs. Bailey, but I really didn't have to go until just now."

"Well," she said, followed by 'tsk,' "I suppose just this once."

"Thank you, ma'am." I had learned half way through the first grade that it was easier to get by if the teacher liked you. Again, as my ma-maw would say, 'the more I trust you, the longer the rope,' which, unfortunately, was followed by, 'of course, that just makes it easier to hang you if you do mess up.' So, there's that.

"You'll have to work extra hard and fast when you get to the room," said Mrs. Bailey. "We are starting our spelling words first thing, and spelling is important."

"Yes, ma'am. I will." In short order, we began marching into the building. I peeled off when we passed the boys room and headed straight for one of the stalls. Eagerly, and with anticipation, I carefully unfolded the note. It read:

> Dear Mark,
>
> I think you are the best boy in our class. You can be my boyfriend if you want. If you also like me, meet me after school under the science windows.
>
> Your Girlfriend (If you like),
> Beth O'Riley

Holy Moly. I had a girlfriend.

I did not catch up with the spelling words when I returned to class. I also did not do the math assignment that followed. Hopefully, I wiped the spittle from the corner of my mouth to keep the drool from running down my chin. I did witness every tick of the minute hand all the way to the bell signaling the end of school.

When Mrs. Bailey released the class I piddled around to make sure Beth left the room before I did. I cleverly watched her out of the corner of my eye. She never glanced in my direction. She did not seem the least bit nervous. By all appearances she seemed perfectly normal, like today was just another day, like she wasn't getting ready to have the most epic, monumental meeting of her nine year old life.

I had to hand it to that girl, she was cool as a cucumber, while I had sweaty pits.

The science windows were on the east side of the school. There were high hedges planted all along the building and the way they were planted and trimmed left about two feet between the hedges and the school. It was a perfect place to hide. I do not remember leaving class, the building or walking to the hedges. Suddenly, I was just there. Face to face with Beth. She was smiling.

"Oh," she said. "You do like me back. I am so relieved."

Now I was really confused. The look in her eyes conveyed nervousness and joy. She had been afraid I didn't like her back? This made no sense. She was Beth O'Riley, fourth, (maybe third) most popular girl in school and I was Mark, Mark, Mark, MarkMarkMarkMark. I did not even have a cool ranking.

"Why wouldn't I like you, Beth? Every boy in school likes you. You're smart, funny and lovely. You have the grace of Audrey Hepburn and the beautiful, old soul of Lauren Bacall," is what I wanted to say. What I think I said was, "I think you're neat." Her piercing green eyes cupped by her smoldering red hair were burning my pupils. To avoid permanently damaging my vision I shifted my gaze to my shoelaces.

"I hear you talking to your friends, and I think you're funny. Also, you tell interesting stories during show and tell. I told my mom I liked you and she said at this age, if you like a boy, you should tell them. She said that will change, though. She also said not to be upset if a boy doesn't like you back because some boys in fourth grade don't like girls yet. She said that will change, too, mostly. I told her you were from Texas and she said that was good because people from Texas are polite. Texas is the friendly state. We were stationed in San Antonio for two years, but I was only three years old and I don't remember. We have a picture of me and my whole family in front of the Alamo. Have you been to the Alamo? I imagine you have."

I was still fathoming that Beth thought I was funny. I would not process the rest of what she said until way later that night. I was operating on pure instinct. I reached out my hand and she took it. I was touching a girl. Slowly I leaned in and pursed my lips. She followed suit. I want to emphasize I was acting on instinct alone with no forethought. The next thing I knew, my eyes were closed, and our lips were pressed together.

And that was that. I had my first kiss.

*　*　*

San Francisco Chronicle
October 13, 1969
Zodiac Killer Warns School Bus Children May
Be Next Victims

San Francisco (AP) – The killer who calls himself 'Zodiac' and boasts of five victims now writes that he wants to add to his death list by halting a school bus so he can "pick off the children as they come bouncing out."

*　*　*

My mom, Ricky's mom and Mrs. Herchfeld sat silently around my mom's kitchen table. All three had their copies of the Chronicle neatly folded in front of them. All three had the look of worry like only a mom can worry. The Zodiac killings, letters and exploits had been almost constant headline news since early August 1969. Now he had threatened to shoot a bus load of children.

Noticing Ricky's mom was almost out of coffee, my mom said, "Do you need more coffee, Mary?"

"No, but thank you, Kay."

"Look at the time," said Mrs. Herchfeld. "The boys will be home soon." Mrs. Herchfeld's son was named Billy, not my friend Billy from school, this was a neighbor named Billy. He was a year younger, didn't like to play football or fly balsa wood gliders from the five and dime or really do anything the rest of us neighborhood boys liked to do. My mom always told me to include Billy in our games even though I told her he didn't really want to play with us. She said we really didn't want to play with him, which was true but I wasn't lying either.

"So, Mary, you'll walk them to and from school tomorrow?" said my mom.

"That's right, I'll meet everyone out front at 8:15," replied Mary. "Ricky is not going to be happy having his mother walk him to school."

"Mark won't like it either, but that is just tough noogies."

"I don't think Billy will mind much," said Mrs. Herchfeld. My mom and Ricky's mom nodded in agreement, the secret understanding nod of moms through the ages.

Mrs. Herchfeld and Ricky's mom left through the kitchen back door just as I came home through the front. I slammed the front door and immediately ran upstairs to change into my play clothes. I wasn't six stairs up before mom shouted, "Mark Alan! Get in here." I froze still on the stairs, my mind racing. "What have I done," I wondered. Mom never used my middle name unless I was in trouble. As far as I could cipher, I had committed no crimes or misdemeanors. Nonetheless I quickly ran back down the stairs and into the kitchen.

My mom looked at me and asked, "Where is your saxophone?" In all the excitement of the day, I had left it at school.

I hung my head and muttered, "I left it at school."

"You can't practice if you leave it at school," she said. "But never mind the sax right now. Sit down, I want to talk to you."

I sat down and mom went about the kitchen getting me a glass of milk and a snack. "Tomorrow morning, Mrs. Kyle will be walking you and a group of children to and from school."

I almost died. Then, I saw the newspaper and read the headline. "Awww, mom," I cried.

"Do not aww mom, me, young man." Mom placed a glass of milk and a plate of celery with peanut butter down in front of me. She also grabbed the paper and moved it to the counter. "This is grownup stuff you do not understand."

This was a disaster. I had held hands and kissed a girl. I had serious pull with the guys and now I was going to have to be walked to and from school by somebody's mom, and even worse, sometimes my mom. I was sure to be the laughingstock of the entire school.

I thought I was well on my way to manhood. Hell, I wasn't sure, but I might have become a man today. I was sure men didn't have their mom walk them to school in the fourth grade. If I had known how to properly cuss, I would have, well, that and if I had no regard for my physical wellbeing because I was pretty convinced that if I cussed around my mom, she would have taken me out.

— ⋅⋅✦✦✦✦⋅⋅ —

Life Magazine
Volume 66 Number 25
June 27, 1969
Faces of the American Dead in Vietnam: One Week's Toll, June 1969

The faces shown on the next pages are the faces of American men killed—in the words of the official announcement of their deaths—"in connection with the conflict in Vietnam." The names, 242 of them, were released on May 28 through June 3 [1969], a span of no special significance except that it includes Memorial Day. The numbers of the dead are average for any seven-day period during this stage of the war.

This issue of Life magazine had been sitting on the nightstand by my mom's side of the bed for four months. It looked newsstand fresh. I think mom read it once and laid it down. It just lay on the nightstand by her bed. I had walked out of my room a couple of times and caught her sitting on the bed, staring at the cover. She wasn't holding it, I don't think it ever moved, she just stared at it.

I was standing in my parent's room staring at the Life cover and listening to my parents argue downstairs in the living room. We lived in base housing constructed in the 1940s. Everything was made from concrete and cinder block. The acoustics were such that every word said above a whisper in the living room bounced upstairs and into my parents' bedroom clear as a bell.

My parents argued consistently and about almost everything from the usual, like money and politics to the more mundane like what to watch on TV. Tonight they were arguing about whether my mom should pack me and our belongings up and move back to Texas while dad was deployed to Vietnam for six months. We were less than a year into our two year stint at Mare Island in Vallejo, California. Dad didn't see the need for mom to move back to Texas and six months later move back to California. I didn't understand the logistics or economics of the argument. I knew mom was worried about dad being killed in Vietnam. I knew she was worried about me being killed by the Zodiac killer. I felt helpless and alone. I sat in my parents' room on my mom's side of the bed, staring at the Life magazine cover and listening as the argument escalated from disagreement to screaming match.

✦✦✦✦✦✦

In the three months since my dad deployed to Vietnam, mom had lost over twenty pounds, dyed her hair platinum blonde and I had turned 10 years old. It was a big birthday for me, I was finally double digit of age. Beth's dad had been transferred to Virginia, so I was once again single but still a legend for being the only boy in fourth grade to have ever, no matter how briefly, had a girlfriend.

When dad went to sea Mom had taken to going out with friends, mainly two other moms whose husbands were also on deployment. One of the other moms had two younger children, a two and a four year old. Mom sat me down one day and told me I was old enough to start babysitting and when they went out, I watched the kids and put them to bed. Most of the time when mom and her friends went out the younger children were brought to our house but occasionally, I went to their place, which was still base housing but a couple of miles away.

I never rested easy when staying away from home. Strange environment, strange night noises, strange bed, did not suit me. I would generally lie awake until I heard my mom and her friends come home. One night, as I stared at the ceiling, I heard the women's voices when they come home but this time they were accompanied by male voices. Usually when I heard my mom's voice I could drift off to sleep, but they were a little more boisterous and the two male voices peaked my curiosity. After a while things quieted down and the only sound coming up the stairs was soft music on the radio. I decided to investigate and slinked quietly down the stairs. About half way down I peeked into the living room and saw my mom, sans blouse, lying on the couch in the arms of a man I had never laid eyes on.

I retraced my steps and returned to bed and lay awake until morning.

＊＊＊＊＊＊

My dad returned from sea midsummer after the fourth grade and was given early orders to our next duty station. We were off to Saudi Arabia. I was excited to be going to such an exotic country until I learned I had to be inoculated against every known disease to mankind and at least five unknown maladies. After ten straight days of inoculations my left arm was swollen as a tick. This was particularly uncomfortable for me as I am left handed, which I told the doctor. Everyday. For each and every shot. This did not matter as military doctors only know how to do things the military way and, in the military, you get your shots in the left arm. Eight days after my last shot and just as my arm was beginning to return to its normal size and color, my dad came home and told us his orders had changed and we would be moving to Maryland. It was of no solace that if a sudden outbreak of malaria or the bubonic plague had broken out around the Chesapeake Bay area, I stood a great chance of being the only survivor.

The fourth grade had been a whirlwind. I had gotten a girl, kissed a girl, lost a girl, turned a double digit age, gained responsibility, lost control and found not only was I not a man, I wasn't wiser by one iota.

THE GAS MASK
By Kelley Baker

nhale!

Inhale!

Inhale!

Mike feels the pressure of the mask around his face.

Inhale!

It grows tighter. The smoke rushes to his lungs.

Inhale!

The smoke goes down deeper. He can't exhale.

Inhale!

The flame burns bright in front of him. His face is getting hot.

Inhale!

He gasps as the smoke fills his lungs. The mask pushes itself harder and harder into his face.

Inhale!

His irritated eyes open wider. Through the eyeholes he sees everyone staring.

Inhale!

His lungs are gasping inwards. He wants to cough but he can't.

Inhale!

The smoke gets thicker. His lungs ache. He has no choice but to inhale. The mask is smashing his face.

Inhale!

His chest hurts. He no longer sees the faces around him. Thoughts of suffocation swirl through his brain.

Inhale!

The pressure on his face. Everything is obscured by the smoke. Don't black out his brain screams!

Inhale!

Mike can't take it anymore. He grabs the mask and with every once of strength he rips it from his face using both hands!

Exhale! Exhale! Exhale!

He coughs out the smoke, gasping for breath. He feels the cool air on his face even though it's a hot day.

"Cool! That was the best time yet." Tim says looking at his watch. "Almost seventy seconds."

Mike doubles over struggling to catch his breath. The mask has left a long red gash where it dug into his face. His eyes are red and beads of sweat appear on the chest of his "Mr. Natural" t-shirt. He tries to focus.

"My turn." Says Beth as she reaches for the mask.

The mask is a World-War-Two era gas mask attached to a water pipe.

Long rubber tubes that look like radiator hoses, attach the mask to the base of the water pipe. You put the mask on, light the bowl, and inhale. The smoke comes rushing through the tubes right into your face.

There's no place for the smoke to go but into your mouth, nose, and eyes. As you inhale the smoke is forced down your lungs.

It's engineering genius. The gas mask gets you stoned quickly, efficiently, and very effectively.

It's the work of Tim, Mike's roommate. As a pot delivery method it has few peers. But there's one downside.

The release valve is broken. Which is why you can't exhale.

When Tim first built this marvelous contraption you inhaled as long as you could and then you calmly turned the release valve on the front of the mask. You were able to exhale as the smoke quickly exited.

Now that feature is broken so as you inhale the rubber outline of the mask seals to your face. The more you inhale the harder it digs in. It sticks so fiercely to your face that you have to pry it off.

Gas masks were originally designed to keep gas out of your lungs. They were developed to combat chemical gas attacks on the battlefield. This one is made of rubber with clear lenses for your eyes and was attached to a canister that filters the air.

Tim removed the canister and attached the hoses to a water pipe.

The water pipe is a marvelous invention in it's own right. The water in the pipe takes the edge off the harsh smoke of whatever it is you put in the bowl.

Beth's already done two hits and is very stoned, but she loves the mask and wants to go again.

"So how do you guys know each other?" Tim asks.

Beth looks over at Mike. "We met at a speech competition. Mike read the funniest speech so I went up afterwards and talked to him."

"Yeah she was there to support her friend who I was reading against." Mike says.

"I'll bet that didn't go over very well. I mean you talking to Mike and all."

"No. She thought he was cute too."

Beth smiles at Mike. He looks at his feet, not used to compliments.

Beth wears her long curly red hair wild and free flowing past her shoulders. Her colorful t-shirts and faded bell-bottoms highlight her slender frame.

Mike moved out of his parent's house at seventeen. Not over any issues or to rebel, he just wants to be on his own. He isn't going to college and is already working so why not? Besides so much is going on in nineteen-seventy-three and he wants to be a part of something. He just doesn't know what.

Tim fires up the bowl. Mike hears the water bubble as Beth inhales and the bowl glows bright red.

Mike wonders how such a small woman can smoke so much pot.

Earlier Beth called her parents in Eugene to let them know she was okay and staying at Mike's parents house. When her father insisted on talking to Mike's parents, Tim got on the phone and played the role of Mike's Dad.

"Hello Bill this is Jim, Mike's Dad. … I'm doing fine … She's not any trouble you have a real nice girl here. … She's sharing a bedroom with my daughter and they seem to get a long just fine. … I understand. We can't be too careful with our daughters can we? … It's no problem at all. Nice to have her here. … Well you too Bill. Thanks. I'll give the phone back to Beth now."

Beth gets back on the phone and assures her father she's being good and will be home tomorrow. She has a bus ticket and Mike will take her to the station in the afternoon.

They all crack up when the phone is finally hung up.

"Wow, I've never played someone's dad before. I must be getting old?" Tim says.

Since Mike moved in with Tim he's smoking more and more pot. He also takes acid and lots of speed so he can keep a job and maintain a party life style.

But he's growing tired of this. He thinks maybe he needs a girlfriend he can go out and do things with instead of sitting around partying with the guys all the time. It's why he invited Beth up to visit. And he really likes her.

Later that evening after drinking and smoking more, Beth and Mike go to bed. Mike's bedroom is behind the kitchen. As the party continues, Beth and Mike can hear everything through the walls.

This is the second night they've slept together, and that's what it's been so far, sleeping. They're both inexperienced, so they get naked and jump in to bed and make out.

Mike thinks he knows what he's supposed to do but has never slept with a woman. His hands fumble around trying to mimic what he's seen in movies.

As cool as Beth looks she isn't sure what to do either.

"Are you sure you're okay with this?" Mike says as he gets on top of her.

"Uh huh."

Mike is trying to put his dick in and it won't go. Is he not hard enough? Is she too dry? Neither of them have a clue. They don't know what to say, or how to talk about it. After a few tries he rolls over on to his back.

"I'm sorry."

"It's okay. We can keep trying."

Beth wants so badly to lose her virginity.

Laying in the dark and looking at the ceiling Mike feels frustrated and alone.

Beth rolls over and puts her hand on his chest. She kisses him. He kisses back. He puts his arm around her and pulls her on top of him.

They attempt to make love multiple times but are unsuccessful.

Thoughts run through both their minds.

"It always looks so easy in the movies."

"I'm so nervous. Why can't he put it inside of me?"

"I think I'm hard but then when I try to put it inside…"

"Maybe he doesn't think I'm attractive?"

"I really like her."

"What's wrong with me that he can't do it?"

"What's wrong with me?"

"I wish my boobs were bigger. Then maybe he'd find me more attractive."

"She is so beautiful. I've never been with anyone like her and I'm screwing it up."

"I hope he doesn't tell his friends that I can't do it?"

"She's probably gonna tell her friends what a loser I am."

In the end they fall asleep.

Beth wakes up first. She looks at him in the early morning light.

This is her last chance before she has to go home. She puts her hand under the covers and reaches for him. Mike is already hard. She kisses him as he opens his eyes. She rolls over on top of him determined. She kisses his lips, his cheek, his neck.

"I need to go to the bathroom." Mike blurts out.

"What?"

"I really have to go to the bathroom. I'll be right back."

Mike gets up and hurries out the door. A few minutes later he's back, and he's no longer hard. He climbs back into bed. He reaches over to kiss her but now she feels awkward.

"I'll be right back." She says as she gets up, puts on a t-shirt and leaves the room. He hears the bathroom door close.

He lies there staring at the ceiling.

"I'm such a loser."

They get stoned before breakfast so they don't have to talk about it.

Before they know it, it's two o'clock. Time to leave for the bus station. Mike wants to drive her all the way home but he's afraid. He's sure her father knows they've been sleeping together.

Beth wants to use the gas mask one more time. It's the only way she can deal with the three-hour bus ride home.

She dons the mask and Mike lights her up. He watches as she inhales. She keeps the mask on for quite a while. When she tears it off her face is bright red. It matches her hair.

One more time becomes three more times.

"We better go." Mike tells her.

Driving to the bus station they make small talk. Even though they spent the weekend together Mike still doesn't know much about her.

Mike and Beth promise each other they'll stay in touch and he'll come down in a few weeks and stay at his sister's so they can have more time together.

They kiss multiple times and when they call out Beth's bus, she turns and walks away. He watches her board the bus then walks out to his car.

What happened to the weekend? Mike can't remember much of anything besides the gas mask and his failures in bed.

The weather's beautiful and Mike had thought about driving her up to Mount Hood or maybe out to Sauvie Island where they could go swimming. But they didn't. They stayed at his house and got stoned.

A wasted weekend in so many ways.

On his drive home, Mike convinces himself that Beth had a lousy time and doesn't want to see him again.

Beth stares out the bus window not seeing the scenery rolling by. She replays the weekend over in her head. Riding home she feels lonely and empty.

When Mike gets home, Tim and a few people he doesn't know are in the living room smoking and laughing. He excuses himself.

He opens the window in his bedroom hoping to get the smell of smoke and an unfulfilled weekend out. He lies on his bed and looks at the ceiling for a long time.

ABDULLAH THE BUTCHER IN GOTHAM
By Mark A. Nobles

"Dibs on Superman," said Teeter.

"You're always Superman," Monk protested.

"Yep," said Teeter. "Because I am Superman.

"Fine, I'm the Flash," said Monk.

"I wanna be Aquaman," piped in Rayburn.

"Aquaman is in the ocean," said Rod with exaggerated exasperation. "There ain't an ocean in a hundred miles of here."

Rayburn countered, "Aquaman can be outta the ocean, Rod."

"Cannot," said Monk.

"Can to," said Rod

"Just pick someone different," pleaded Monk.

"If Teeter always gets to be Superman, I oughta be able to be Aquaman," said Rayburn.

"Just how is Aquaman supposed to get from the ocean all the way up here?" said Teeter. "Like Rod said, it's got to be a hundred miles, at least."

"We ain't in Alvarado, Teeter, we're in Gotham," said Rayburn.

"Metropolis," corrected Teeter.

"Dang it, Teeter, we're always in Metropolis, you know I'm gonna be Batman, and I want to be in Gotham." Rayburn

"Fine, but just this once. Never again," said Teeter.

"Not just this once, we can be in Gotham sometimes."

"Just this once or never."

"That's not fair, Teeter," said Rayburn.

Teeter shrugs.

"Just say okay," said Monk. "He won't stick to it."

"Okay," begrudged Rayburn.

All eyes turn to Chick. There was tension. Definite tension. Everyone knew what was coming but fervently hoped it would not.

"Abdullah the Butcher," Chick said defiantly.

All together: "Dang." "Not again, Chick." "Every stinking time." "Man."

"How many times do we have to explain that Abdullah the Butcher is not a superhero, Chick," said Monk.

"Is too," protested Chick. "Well," Chick changed his mind, "he's not a superhero, he's a supervillain, and that's better." Chick took a few steps out of the circle of boys and dropped into a crouch position, arms extended, ready to wrestle anyone or even all of the good guys.

"Jeeze," Rod exclaimed.

Monk elbowed Rod in the ribs, "Don't say that or I can't hang out with you." Monk was Preacher Bonds youngest child. Never mind that his two oldest brothers were the biggest pot dealers in Johnson County. They weren't allowed to hang out with folks who took the Lord's name in vain either. Even Monk's older brothers insisted on clean language from their friends and customers, who were pretty much one and the same. In a small town, it was hard to hide who was doing what with who. The teachers at the high school joked that you could tell the potheads from the binge drinkers by their language. The cleaner the language, the bigger the pothead.

"Why we got to do this every time, Chick?" Rayburn asked.

"Cause ya'll are stubborn and won't let me be a wrestling supervillain," Chick stated rather matter of factly. He began to ominously stomp around the circle of boys, who were all now facing outward. "I've come for you, Superman," Chick said in an unknown accent that he believed sounded Sudanese, which was the backstory for Abdullah. It really sounded like what a boy who had barely ever been outside Johnson County imagined sounded middle eastern.

"What the hell are you doing, Chick?" said Teeter.

"I am Abdullah the Butcher!" Chick screamed. "The Madman from the Sudan and I'm going to use my superpower of the Running Elbow Drop to crush you, Superman."

"That's not a superpower, Abdullah," Teeter said, heavy sarcasm on Abdullah.

"Then counter with your super strength, or fly away in shame for my superpowers are greater than yours!" and with that, Chick lunged at Teeter, threw him to the dirt, stepped back and executed a perfect Running Elbow Drop to Teeter's chest. The air whisked from Teeter's lungs with a mighty blast.

"Ohhh!" Monk, Rod, and Rayburn screamed. "Damn," added Rod.

"That's it," said Monk, "I gotta go home, I can't play with ya'll, Rod ruined it," and with that, he double-timed it towards home.

"Wait, Monk," Rod pleaded. He left the circle and took a few steps towards Monk. "I'm sorry, but," he looked back to Teeter and Chick laying on the ground, "Did you see that? Even your dad would have cursed a little."

Chick was feeling his oats, "Where you going in such a hurry, Flash? Come back and climb in the ring with Abdullah the Butcher."

"I'm not allowed to play with sinners or foreigners," shouted Monk.

"We're all sinners, Flash," said Chick, "your daddy says so every Sunday!" Chick was feeling his oats and on a roll. "Besides, Superman in the dirt over here is from Krypton, Aquaman is from the ocean…"

"Atlantis," corrected Rayburn.

Chick turned to Rayburn, "What?"

"Aquaman is from Atlantis," said Rayburn, "it's in the ocean but a pacific place in the ocean, Atlantis." Rayburn had a problem saying specific.

"Whatever," Chick waived Rayburn off and turned back to Monk, "Atlantis is not in America, let alone Texas, and you can play with them. Why can't you play with Abdullah the Butcher, the mad man from the Sudan!"

"You leave my daddy out of this, Chick. At least I have a daddy, you're crazy, that's why your daddy left. I'm not supposed to even play with you because my daddy says divorce is a sin and your momma is either a fornicator or didn't put her husband at the head of the household. Either way, we only play with you because you won't leave us alone and Teeter says it would be rude to tell you to leave." After issuing that mouthful Monk was a little winded.

Chick stood frozen in the moment. Slowly his fists clenched and he let out a yell that can best be described as a war cry and began to run straight at Monk.

"Shit is on now," said Rod. Both Rod and Rayburn lit out after Chick.

Poor Teeter was only now catching his breath and climbing to his feet.

Monk stood frozen like a spotlit deer as Chick screamed towards him. Rod and Rayburn had no chance of intercepting Chick and thwarting the waylay. When Chick was about five feet from Monk he went airborne and executed a clean leaping clothesline. The force of the blow from Chick's forearm to Monk's throat and chest knocked the air and consciousness clean out of him. Monk was out before his legs buckled.

Chick blew right past Monk, landed on the dirt in a clean tuck and roll, then bounded to his feet. He was both kinds of mad, bull and hatter. Chick turned and faced the boys, red-faced and breathing deep. He resumed his wrestling crouch.

"Take it easy, Chick," said Rod. "We were only playing."

"Then why can't I play the way I want to play," Chick seethed. "What does it matter to ya'll if I want to be Abdullah?"

Teeter had regained his feet and most of his senses. "Those are just the rules, Chick."

"I want to know who made these rules. Bring them to me!" shouted Chick.

Everyone just stood and stared, except for Monk. He was still out like a light.

"Maybe my momma can't buy me every comic every time a new one comes out but I can watch wrestling on channel 11 with my gramps. It's the same kinda stories, you morons! Good versus evil. Right versus wrong. Truth, justice and the American way. Don't ya'll get it?"

They didn't get it but Chick went on anyway, "Kennedy said, not just three months ago, 'we shall pay any price, bear any burden, meet any hardship, support any friend, oppose any foe to assure the survival and success of liberty.'" He paused, waiting to see if a light would go off in any of them. Any one of them. "Good needs evil or there are no stories. I may be different, but I am real, and ya'll need me."

Monk made a noise and attempted to roll over. He was slowly regaining consciousness. Rod, Rayburn, and Teeter went to attend to him.

Chick turned and walked home.

BLUE BOWLING BALL DAY
By Kelley Baker

On the morning of July 16, 1969, Apollo 11 astronauts, Neil Armstrong, Buzz Aldrin, and Michael Collins sit atop a Saturn Five rocket at the Kennedy Space Center. The three-stage three-hundred-sixty-three-foot rocket will use its seven-point-five million pounds of thrust to propel them into space and into history.

The engines fire and Apollo 11 clears the tower. Roughly twelve minutes later, the crew is in Earth orbit.

When your birthday's in the summer most people forget about it. If your birthday's in July it's even worse. No one's ever around. My friends are on vacation, out of town, at camp, or just doin' other things.

I'm jealous of kids who have birthdays during the school year 'cause they get to have parties at school and all the kids sing happy birthday to 'em.

Before Mom started working my birthday felt special. Dad usually had to work so Mom would take us to Oaks Park where we'd go on the rides all day. One time we went to Sauvie Island to swim. Those were fun birthdays but now that she works my birthday is just another day.

Sometimes we go out to dinner, if they can afford it. I get a cake and a couple presents but it's not like it was when my birthday was special.

After traveling 240,000 miles in 76 hours, Apollo 11 enters a lunar orbit on July 19.

But this year is gonna be different. I told Mom and Dad what I want and they said, "Okay". It's just one present cause it's kind of expensive, but I really want it!

My own personal bowling ball. And I get to pick it out.

I've been bowling for a couple years and I joined a junior league team with my friend Tim. He has his own ball and a little towel to keep his hand dry. It's pretty cool. There are four of us on the team. Every Saturday morning I walk down to Tim's house and his mom drives us to the bowling alley. We bowl while she watches and buys us Cokes and stuff.

I'm not the best bowler, but that's okay 'cause I have a high handicap. They add your handicap to whatever you bowl and that's your final score. The other guys on our team have really low handicaps 'cause I haven't been bowling as long as they have. I'm also the youngest.

Last year I won my first trophy. It was for the highest game with handicap.

I bowled a really great game, better than I ever have. I bowled a one-eighty-seven and then they added my handicap and that made it a two-forty-two.

I really need my own bowling ball so I can bowl better.

*"Everything's going just swimmingly. Beautiful!" Michael Collins -
over the radio to Mission Control.*

Every Saturday I walk all over the alley looking for the right
ball. Even though I'm thirteen my hands are pretty good sized.
Finding a ball with finger holes that fit me is a big problem.

If they don't fit right you can't throw very well. If they're
too loose you can drop the ball before you mean to throw it. I've
seen that before. And if they're too tight it's harder to make the
ball go where you want cause your fingers stick. I've seen a lot
of gutter balls cause the finger holes were too tight.

There is one ball I like, but since all the balls are black it's
really hard to find it every week. Sometimes other people take
it before I get there. That's why I need my own.

*At 1:46 p.m., the lunar module Eagle, with Neil Armstrong and
Buzz Aldrin aboard separates from the command module, Michael
Collins stays behind.*

I didn't sleep at all last night. Now I have to wait for Dad
to get home from work.

It's a nice day and I could go out and play but I'm too
"wound up" as Mom would say. I want Dad to hurry up and get
home. I know it's Sunday but my Dad sells cars. Sometimes he
works Saturday and Sunday but then he gets a couple days off
during the week. Today he's just meeting a customer to deliver
a car.

Mom says the bowling alley doesn't open until noon anyway.

I'm sitting in my room listening to the radio and working
on one of my model cars. It's a nineteen sixty-six Corvair and
I'm gluing the front suspension together. I'm trying to be careful
with the cement cause it's really easy to squeeze too much out
and then it's a mess and it dries really fast. Then it looks bad.

Dad's home! I run downstairs so we can go, but he wants to have lunch first. Why does everything have to take forever!

Two hours later, the Eagle begins its descent to the lunar surface. Armstrong looks out the window and sees the automatic landing system taking Eagle to a rocky field. He takes control of the spacecraft, steering it down on to the southwestern edge of the Sea of Tranquility with just seconds of fuel to spare.

Finally we drive to Valley Lanes out in Beaverton. I bowl at Grand Central but my parents bowl at Valley and Dad's already talked to the guys there.

The parking lot is empty.

Walking into the bowling alley it's really weird. I've never been in a quiet bowling alley. There's nobody here except the two guys who run the place and they're sitting at a table watching TV.

Bill, the short fat bald guy, says hi to Dad as he gets up and off we go to the bowling ball display area.

Apollo Eleven is on the moon. Armstrong immediately radios to Mission Control: "Houston, Tranquility Base here. The Eagle has landed."

I thought I knew what I wanted but now looking at all these different bowling balls I'm not sure. There are red ones, white ones, and some have different patterns on them.

Bill and Dad talk while I look around. Then I see it! A blue bowling ball.

It's not all blue cause that would be like a girls bowling ball and I certainly don't want that. I have enough trouble just talking to girls and if I were to have a solid blue bowling ball I'm not sure what I'd do.

It's black but it has all this blue stuff in it, sort of like blue clouds or blue flames or something.

I can see it now spinning down the alley, a black and blue blur. That's the one I want.

This is gonna help my scores I just know it. I'll finally have a lower handicap like the other guys.

I tell Dad this is the one. He looks at it for a moment, asks if I'm sure, and when I say yes, he tells Bill we'll take it!

At 10:39 p.m., five hours ahead of the original schedule, Armstrong opens the hatch of the lunar module. As he makes his way down the module's ladder, a television camera attached to the craft beams the signal back to Earth, where hundreds of millions of people watch in great anticipation.

I wanna bowl with it today but Bill says he has to measure my fingers for the holes, drill them out, and do some finish work. The ball won't be ready until next week.

Next Week! I can't wait until next week! I thought I was getting it today.

"That'll be fine." Says Dad

Bill measures my fingers so he can make the holes.

"Do you want your name on this? Bill asks.

I nod.

"How come no one's bowling?"

"Everyone's home watching the moon landing."

"Hey Dad can we bowl a couple games as long as we're here? It's so empty we could probably pick any lane we want."

"No. We need to get home."

"Why do we need to get home? It's my birthday. Why can't I bowl a couple games?"

Dad shakes his head no.

As we walk out of the bowling alley I see Bill go back over to the table and sit down and watch the TV.

"What's the big deal? It's just a dumb old moon landing…"

When we get home Mom has our old black and white TV on.

"How'd it go?" She asks.

"Dad wouldn't let me bowl." I say as I head off to my room.

On July 20, 1969, Neil Armstrong is the first human to step out on to the surface of the moon.

"One small step for man. One giant leap for mankind." - Neil Armstrong

The Apollo program was a costly and labor intensive endeavor, involving an estimated 400,000 engineers, technicians and scientists, and costing $24 billion (close to $100 billion in today's dollars).

Drilling out my bowling ball takes one guy about an hour and cost eight dollars. I'm sitting in my room, dejected. What a lousy birthday this is turning out to be.

At least I got a blue bowling ball.

THE SHADOW BOYS
By Mark A. Nobles

The shadow boys live in the Fort Worth & Denver City rail yard amongst the empty cars and tool shacks. When the freight men shuffle the cars, or ransack the shacks for parts, tools or machinery, the boys scatter like rats in a woodpile. The freight men seldom give chase because the boys are far too quick, but if a boy is caught off guard or proves to slow, the freight men will beat him for sport. The FW & DC yard sits due east of Hell's Half Acre by only a couple of stone throws.

The shadow boys frequent the Acre to steal, beg, and sometimes find gainful, if not always lawful, employment, or work the rough trade for gey cats and quickly duck back to the yard for safety, if need be.

The shadow boys come from all points but mostly from the west. Some are orphans, some have been abandoned, most are runaways fleeing no longer bearable lives. The boys make their way to Fort Worth by foot, rail or any means available. Most come from the west because Fort Worth is a beacon for West Texas dreams, but its underbelly is hard and mean and most of those dreams starve out or are brutally beaten to extinction.

In Fort Worth, the cattle drives have ended but the cattle still come, by rail nowadays, not by hoof. The Armour and Swift slaughter factories on the north side leak the stink of death and rot throughout the city. The greasy smoke from the rendering and the effluent into the drainage pipes make the city smell like something Yama dropped in his toilet after a bad meal.

Matilda saw the strip of cloth on the back fence but was unable to get away until the last man had left Harlow's bawdy house two hours later. The strip of tattered calico hanging from the picket meant one of the shadow boys was in need. Harlow, the house madam, had picked up Matilda from an orphan train eight months prior. Matilda had been scooped off the streets of Baltimore on her way home from spending the night in a back alley off Aliceanna Street. Her father had been killed when she was four and her mother had turned to prostitution to keep food on the table. By the time Matilda was nine the men who came to the tenement in Fells Point began to turn their attention to Matilda and she took to sleeping in the streets to avoid the advances.

The orphan trains were supposed to deliver children to families or Christian homes in the Midwest and South, but Harlow paid a middle-aged couple with a morphine addiction to go to the station, say they were married, willing and able to care for the girl. It was easy pickings and cheap labor.

Matilda had managed to avoid prostitution in Baltimore only to be shipped halfway across the country and put to work on her back in Hell's Half Acre. She left Harlow's house out the back door and exited the yard through the rickety picket gate, turned left in the alley and walked the hundred yards to a vacant lot. Red and Milky sat in the dirt. Red was bare-chested as he had taken off his shirt to wrap around Milky's injured hand. Milky had pretty near sliced his left thumb clean off attempting to open a can of peaches with a rock and a razor blade. Don't bother looking for the logic in opening a can of peaches with a rock and a razor blade for there is none but don't judge him either because logic is rare in the mind of a three-quarter starved twelve-year-old boy's line of thinking.

The point here is Milky's thumb hung to his hand by the top layer of skin only. Red looked to Matilda with worry in his eye as she walked up on the boys.

"What happened?" asked Matilda. Though mostly obscured by his fire colored hair, Matilda could see enough of Red's eyes to know Milky was hurt worse than the usual scrape or sprain.

"His thumb is cut bad," said Red. "It is hanging to his hand. It is a clean slice with a razor."

Matilda stood over Milky. He looked up at her, his good eye bloodshot and filled with tears, his other eye, as usual, was cloudy, white and dead. Matilda shuddered. She still had the capacity to shudder when looking at a soul in pain.

"Let's take him to Harlow, though if it is as bad as you say, ain't likely she can do much but go ahead and take it clean off," said Matilda.

Smelling of blood, sweat and piss, Milky screamed and kicked at the ground. Red wrestled him to his feet and calmed him down. Red could do that to people, this was an ability of Red's Matilda greatly admired but never showed. The trio walked in silence back to Harlow's.

As they entered Harlow's backyard, Red and Milky stopped short of the wooden steps leading up to the back door. Matilda continued, alone, into the house. When she entered the kitchen, Tweet, one of the older girls, almost seventeen, was removing a whistling copper kettle from the stove. The steaming whistle covered the sound of Matilda's entrance, and her sudden appearance made Tweet jump a little. "Gracious, girl, you startled me," said Tweet in her high-pitched voice.

Matilda continued into the kitchen and stared at the door leading to the hallway. "Sorry, didn't mean to." Matilda rung her hands and turned to Tweet. "Have you seen Mrs. Harlow?" To the best of anyone's knowledge, Harlow was not nor had she ever been married, but she insisted on being addressed as Missus.

"Haven't seen her but sure as hell heard her screaming at a John mere seconds ago," said Tweet. She was pouring hot water into a cup through a strainer of tea leaves. "Would you like some tea? I made plenty of water."

"Yes, I would, but no thank you, I have a favor to ask Mrs. Harlow and I'm a might jumpy. After, though, for sure."

Looking up from pouring the cup of tea Tweet saw Red and Milky standing in the backyard. Red looked anxious and Milky looked pale. "Lordy, Matilda," she said, "You are sure enough pushing your luck bringing more of those boys to this back door." She turned to face Matilda. "You gone waste all your money helping those wastrels. Harlow doesn't give you near your value and charges you through the roof to patch them up."

Matilda dropped her eyes to the worn wooden floor and her chin to her chest. Harlow always made a show of not wanting to help the boys. She would scream and throw a commotion whenever they showed up to the back, once she smacked Matilda hard across her temple. She would then make it known to the rest of the house how much money she would take from Matilda's earnings for the week.

What no one knew was that a week after Matilda had stepped off the Orphan Train, Harlow had come to her room and told her to watch for the strip of cloth signal from the boys, and to bring them in if they really needed help or care. If they were faking or panhandling, Matilda was to shoo them away and tell Harlow who they were so they would be blackballed from ever coming back, but if they were truly in need, Matilda was to bring them to the house. She didn't want to be known as a soft touch and make no mistake, Harlow was not soft. She only stood 5' 2" but no man, no matter how drunk, ornery, or full of himself ever felt big or bad enough to mess with Harlow.

Matilda stood in the kitchen gathering gumption to go look for Harlow. As it happened, she did not have to step foot. Harlow came storming into the kitchen screaming bloody hell, "That gotdamn, egg-sucking, rat bastard!" Harlow could string together cuss words better than Preacher Norris could talk money out of the congregation's pockets.

Harlow was toting two Gladiola flour sacks stuffed full of nine shot riddled quail. As she entered the kitchen she threw one bag forward and sent it sliding across the floor spilling bloody quail at Matilda's feet. "Imagine having the gall, the GALL, to pay me with quail!" Harlow stopped to draw breath, darting her eyes from Tweet to Matilda. Both girls knew they were not expected to answer the question. "That is some bullshit, right there."

Harlow stood, hands on her hips, letting the blood drain from her flushed face. Matilda turned and walked to the back door, opened it and motioned for the two boys to approach.

"Oh, good lord a mercy," exclaimed Harlow. "More peckers come to cause me trouble. Let that be a hard lesson learned, girls. Peckers mean trouble."

Red and Milky entered, Harlow saw the blood-soaked shirt wrapped around Milky's hand, walked over and began to gently expose the wound.

She unfolded the last piece of cloth and softly said, "Lordy, child." Matilda and Tweet squeezed their eyes shut as if trying to push out the sight of Milky's mangled hand from their mind, but neither flinched, they had both seen enough bordello brawls to lose their squeamish.

"Ooo wee, child. There is no saving that thumb," said Harlow, shaking her head. "You got a bad eye and now you only have nine fingers." She raised up and began to walk out of the room. "You got parts going bad and falling off one by one. Pretty soon there won't be nothing left of you but a Cheshire smile." Reaching the doorway she turned and addressed the group. "Heat a butcher knife red hot, fetch some shine and get that boy passed out drunk. Call me when everything is set."

Matilda walked to a cabinet drawer to the left of the sink, it made a weak, small creak when she pulled it open. She reached in and withdrew the butcher knife. Tweet went to an old red pie safe, opened it, reached in, and grabbed a mason jar of moonshine. The four shelves of the pie safe were lined, three deep, with almost identical jars of shine.

Matilda placed the knife on the open gas flame of the right back burner of the stove. Tweet unscrewed the mason jar and placed it on the table in front of Milky.

"Cain't he have a glass?" asked Red.

"Are you gonna wash it after he's through? I do enough dishes around here." Tweet wasn't being mean, just practical. "He needs to drink this whole jar and what he don't finish, I will."

The four stood around the kitchen table in silence waiting for the knife to heat up, Milky gulping the moonshine best he could. He choked once and almost heaved. Matilda walked to the pantry and returned with a loaf of bread, broke off a heel and gave it to Milky. "Maybe if you dip it the shine will go down easier." In another part of town, four children gathered around a kitchen table would look as American as apple pie, but in another part of town, they wouldn't be drinking shine, and about to cut off a thumb. That kind of thing only happened in Hell's Half Acre.

Matilda kept one eye on the blade. Harlow walked in just as it began glowing bright orange. Milky was about as gone as the two-thirds empty mason jar. "Close your eyes son, this won't hurt a bit," said Harlow. There was a thick, blue oven mitt with embroidered daisies hanging by the stove. She grabbed it, put in on her right hand and reached for the knife.

✦✦✦✦✦

Napoleon, all elbows, and knees, ran breakneck down the tracks. He was late for work and that would not do. The wind blowing through the discarded sheet metal, trees, and loose debris sounded like an orchestra tuning to b flat. Napoleon was tall for his fifteen years. The shadow boys called him Napoleon because he was self-conscious of his permanently clenched, twisted, and disfigured left hand and always hid it in his shirt. When his father saw the birth defect, he loaded Napoleon and his mother in the wagon, drove them the thirty-nine miles from Peaster to Fort Worth, and abandoned them in the Acre. His mother dropped him off at the Texas Children's Home Society, a home for orphans, from which he promptly ran away. His mother disappeared into the bowels of the Acre. His father went back to Peaster, remarried and had a healthy brood.

Napoleon was one of the few boys to have a job and he was proud of the fact. He always kept a nickel or at least a penny in his pocket to show the advantages of employment and bragged about being able to afford eating fresh, unspoiled food.

Napoleon hit Seventeenth Street at a full gallop heading towards Rusk. He turned right on Rusk, and although winded, picked up his pace, he had to be at the Waco Tap saloon in less than five minutes and it was an eight minute journey at his current stride.

Napoleon's job at the Waco Tap consisted of sweeping, cleaning, and mopping up blood and beer but if he was late, Tips the bartender would replace him, quick as a lick, with one of the rum bums who was always hanging around looking for free drinks. If he lost his job he would have to hustle and steal for his bread like the other shadow boys. Plus, he would surely lose his fiancé, Essa.

To be honest, Essa was Napoleon's third fiancé in less than eight months, although, at five weeks, she had lasted the longest. There is also the fact that Essa had absolutely no idea Napoleon existed. She cleaned the rooms upstairs at the Waco Tap and ran errands for the soiled doves working there. Occasionally, she handled overflow customers. Essa was twelve and Tips the bartender paid her mostly in alcohol and laudanum. She barely knew who she was, let alone Napoleon. She was Napoleon's fiancé in his mind only. In fact, most of Napoleon's life was a fiction. Tips the bartender rarely paid him for working. He stole to earn his keep like the rest of the shadow boys. His ten hours at the Waco Tap was a roof over his head and sometimes he got to sleep in the storeroom. He was safer at the saloon, even with the nightly knife fights, than he was in the train yard or on the streets.

Napoleon ran up the back alley to the Waco Tap and into the propped open back door. He was still moving at a brisk clip when he ran, chest first, into a big bass drum. He was whacked back and dropped to his knees, the collision knocking all the breath from his lungs.

A booming voice came from behind the drum, "Watch where you're goin' kid." A giant man in a tattered tuxedo, bald, with a bushy gray beard, carried the drum, stepped around Napoleon and continued on his way. Three men in matching tuxedoes followed closely behind the giant. Two carried trumpet cases and the third toted a tenor sax, still strapped around his neck. The first trumpet muttered, "Excuse me," as he passed, the second trumpet said nothing, and the sax player thumped Napoleon on his temple with the bell of his instrument as he passed.

Napoleon rose from his knees, rubbed his smarting temple, and walked into the backroom of the Waco Tap. It smelled of rejected prayers, grain alcohol, and broken dreams with a heaping dollop of despair. Tips the bartender stood in the middle of the room, red faced screaming at another man, wearing a white tuxedo. The white tuxedo man was also red faced and screaming. The blue blood vessels on his bald head popped in his temples and skull, looking like the Tarantula map of Fort Worth. There seemed to be a disagreement on payment for services. The band was going home and Tips the bartender was incensed. He saw Napoleon slinking by, "Clear the empties off the tables, then get to mopping, boy!" Tips the bartender wasn't yelling at Napoleon, per se, he was just hyped from his altercation with the bandleader. Napoleon got a large tray to hold the empties, grabbed a dirty rag, stuck it in his back pocket, and went into the saloon to get to work, still out of breath and now with a headache to boot.

Two hours later, Napoleon was mopping the floor in front of the bar, being careful not to trip up any stumble drunks. He mopped this particular stretch of the Waco Tap more than all the others combined. From his position in front of the bar, he could see the upstairs balcony reflected in the long mirror behind the bar. It was his best vantage point to catch a glimpse of Essa as she came and went from the rooms, without seeming to stare.

He noticed a table of rodeo clowns, all with cheeks full of chew, spitting all over the floor. He decided to go to the backroom to fetch a spittoon or two in the hopes the clowns would use them. In his experience, they likely would not. Rodeo clowns don't give two shits. The door to the backroom was midway along the east wall, under the balcony, just as Napoleon walked under the balcony and reached for the door handle, he heard a scream, followed by the sound of snapping lumber, and a sickening thud. Napoleon turned to see Essa sprawled on the floor. Splinters of the broken balcony littered around her body and her head perpendicular to her right shoulder. She had fallen through the rail and landed headfirst.

"You dirty son of a bitch!" screamed Rosie, one of the upstairs working girls.

"Bitch would not move out of my way," retorted a large, well dressed, man.

Tips the bartender came around the bar. No one had made a move to even check if Essa was still alive. "Tips, this bastard, right here was mad because I wouldn't give him his money back.

Hellfire, I blew him for ten minutes, it ain't my fault he got a limp pecker."

As Tips the bartender took the stairs two at a time, Napoleon approached Essa. Reaching her, he knelt and put his face close to hers. They were nose to nose.

There is a certain smell to a person's breath when they are moments from death. It is low and pungent. If it were a color it would be a deep, navy blue, just a whisker lighter than black. Napoleon feels and smells Essa's last breath. He rises to his feet and walks slowly up the stairs, holding the mop in his good hand, his deformed hand in his shirt.

The table of rodeo clowns rises to their feet. "Don't that beat all," said one. He then spits a mouth full of translucent brown tobacco juice on the floor.

Reaching the top of the stairs, Napoleon let lose a guttural scream, raising the mop above his head, he runs towards the well dressed man. Tips the bartender turns, steps aside as if to let him by, but as he passes, Tips the bartender trips Napoleon, and he falls, sprawling out on the deck. The well dressed man walks up and kicks Napoleon in the head. He then pivots, raises his right leg and slams his boot heel square in the back of Napoleon's one good hand, crushing sixteen of its twenty-seven bones.

Napoleon woke in the alley behind the Waco Tap. He had blacked out after the kick to the head. He had pissed his pants, had caked blood from his right ear down his neck, and his good hand was swollen three times normal size.

The sun was not yet above the horizon, but shadows were growing. A drizzling rain washed the soot from the air and coated everything in what looked like black newspaper ink. The setting moon reflected in one of the rain filled ruts running down the alley. The reflection slowly crawled into the morning traffic on Rusk Street. A cat drank from a pan filled with rain until a rat, half again bigger than the scrawny cat, chased it away.

◆◆◆◆◆◆

Red wasn't good at waiting. He never knew what to do with his body, he felt awkward and conspicuous unless he was moving with purpose. After Harlow amputated Milky's thumb, she told Red to go to the vacant lot two days later at sundown, and Matilda would deliver fresh bandages and iodine. Red had come early. He shuffled his feet like a marionette controlled by a puppeteer with delirium tremens.

"You ain't supposed to be here, yet," said Matilda, approaching Red from behind.

Matilda had come down the alley and Red had expected her to come up. He quickly swiveled and faced her. "You startled me a might."

"Harlow sent me out to get sundries for the girls and bandages and iodine to leave here. She said you wouldn't be here until dark."

"I was hoping to catch you," said Red.

"Ain't nobody catching me, Red." Matilda put one bag down and began rustling through the other for the bandages and iodine.

"Thank you for helping get Milky fixed up," said Red.

Matilda did not look up from her search. "It ain't for sure that stump won't get gangrenous and kill him anyway," said Matilda. She found the iodine and handed the small, brown bottle to Red.

"Thanks." Red examined the bottle, it was corked at the top and had a large skull and crossbones on the front and back. "Who would be daft enough to drink iodine," said Red.

"You never know the weeds that grow in other peoples minds, Red." Matilda gave up searching the bag for the bandages and turned her attention to the one on the ground. "Where in tarnation are those bandages."

"Mama's Boy got a real job at O.B. Macaroni," Red blurted with some excitement.

"I don't know him, do I? There it is," she said as she drew her hand out of the burlap bag. "Bandages," she said, holding them out.

"Thank you," Red said as he took the bandages. "I don't think you know him, but the point is he said he could get me on. Get me a real job."

"That would be great, Red," said Matilda. "I'm happy for you."

"With a job, I could afford to get a room, and save enough to get a proper little cottage. It might take a while, but I was hoping after I got on my feet, we could be together, Matilda. Start a family, live like real folks." All the blood rushed to Red's head, he became flushed. "I been prayin' on it."

Matilda picked up the bag on the ground and looked Red straight in the eyes so he would listen. "Prayers are just dreams, Red. When I got taken from my momma and put on the train, I told them fella's I had a family. I wasn't no orphan. I prayed and prayed someone would listen to me. I prayed the whole time, when the train pulled away and my life, my family, became smaller and smaller, so did my prayers, until they was gone."

The boys huddled around the fire in a small patch of mesquite to the southeast of the rail yards. The fire was below ground level and smokeless so as not to attract unwanted attention. A shadow boy, whose name no one remembered, dug a Dakota fire hole long ago. The story goes he dug it overnight with his bare hands and a piece of glass from a broken beer bottle. He dug the Dakota fire hole, which consists of a one foot deep pit connected to a six inch tunnel running off to the side to provide air to the fire, after a pack of hoboes had been attracted to the boy's fire the night before and had beaten him badly and killed his sister. As long as dry wood is used, little to no smoke is produced and if the wind is blowing in the direction of the tunnel, the fire will burn long and hot. The boys were roasting a fresh dog carcass and two quail Red had brought from Harlow.

"I can't remember my momma, no more," said Nine-Toe.

"At least you knew her and had something to forget," said Crooked. "I never had a momma."

"Everyone has a momma, just some momma's don't want their kids," said Falldown. "Besides, sometimes forgettin' is better. My momma carried a fire poker like a walking cane and used to beat us kids with it for no reason."

"My momma was good," said Nine-Toe. "She had blue eyes, like me."

"Your eyes are brown," said Falldown.

"I don't think Red is coming back tonight," said Crooked. "It is late. We best scatter."

"Likely so," agreed Falldown.

The boys divvied up the dog and quail. Crooked stood but did not straighten from being hunched over the fire. His arthritis twisted his spine and hitched his gate so he always looked as if he were walking at a forty-five-degree angle. He headed north into the moonlight.

Falldown stood and headed east. Nine-Toe stared into the pit for several minutes before standing, kicking enough dirt into the pit to extinguish the fire, and headed south.

⁘ ◆◆◆ ⁘

The moon is a waxing gibbous, two days shy being full. Stratus clouds hang near motionless in a breezeless, black sky.

Red had been walking the tracks heading southeast for hours. He felt the vibration in the crossties long before the light from the train becomes visible. He quickened his pace. In the moonlight, the smoke from the boiler billowed, swirled, and disappeared as if it never existed.

Matilda dreamed of Baltimore, her father, still alive, and two brothers. She could smell the crab cakes her mother made on Sundays, hear the 'tink' of her father tapping his pipe on his brass ashtray, and feel the rhythm of her brothers' breathing as they napped in the corner of the living room. Matilda only allowed herself emotions in her dreams, but it made the waking world all the more dead.

Crooked climbed the lone live oak in the rail yard and perched himself betwixt the fork of two large branches. His back gave him no peace. He could only drift off lying on his belly, almost bear hugging the limb. From his vantage, Crooked could see the stacks of the meatpacking plants on the north side curling smoke into the sky twenty-four hours a day.

Harlow sat at her writing desk with the house ledger open, pen in hand. The house was only silent between five and eight in the morning. In these quiet times, Harlow balanced the books, listened to the gears of the grandfather clock rhythmically turn, and allowed herself to look old and tired. Seven envelopes sat neatly stacked to the right of the ledger, already precisely addressed. One for the gas, one for the police, one for the prosecutor, one for the grocer, one for the doctor, one for the florist and one for the Texas Children's Home and Aid Society.

Nine-Toe walked the back alleys of the Acre, looking for drunks to roll or gey cats to ply the rough trade. He slept only during daylight.

Tweet lay on a bed of red coals, her flesh sizzling and cracking, her body weightless but paralyzed, her mouth twisted but silent. She would wake from the dream in thirty seconds and examine her body for burns. There would be none, of course, for dreams only scar the mind, not the body. When she laid her head back on the pillow she knew she would dream the dream again. She always did. In wake or sleep, Tweet lived an ongoing nightmare.

Milky slept soundly under the stacks of sheet metal and lumber by the tool shop in the Fort Worth Denver City rail yard. His hand, freshly bandaged, ached and throbbed but he had grown used to the discomfort. Tomorrow he planned on tracking down Napoleon to learn how he managed to survive with only one good hand.

Falldown slept fitfully in the culvert running east of the rail yard. The other shadow boys thought him daft for sleeping in a place where hobos traveled night and day and rats woke you every hour or two by taking a bite out of your hand or cheek.

Napoleon floated facedown the Clear Fork branch of the Trinity River, his arms spread out welcoming, like Christ. His body so bloated his clothes had all split off except a portion of his right pant leg still encircling his ankle. He bobbed in the water like a cork float on a cane pole.

I'LL BE OKAY
By Kelley Baker

Don't tell anyone but I've fallen a couple times. My balance isn't so good anymore.

I can still get on my knees to jack up a car to fix a tire or set the lift so I can change the oil, it's just harder getting back up. My knees don't work like they used to. I need something to hang on to. Unless Virgil and Billy are around, then I get up without help. I don't want them to see me like this. It's harder now, but I still do it. I have to.

I've always loved cars. I love working on 'em. It makes you feel good when you fix a car and people appreciate it. I like being appreciated but I like working on cars better. My hands hurt so it's not always easy and I been forgettin stuff.

Some people say when you get older you get wiser. I don't think that's true. I use to be able to just listen to a car and tell you what's wrong with it. Not anymore. The new cars are harder to work on and I never learned about computers so I work on the old ones. They don't have computers.

I always wanted to build hot rods. That's why I started hangin out at Virgil's. He worked on hot rods and racecars and customs too. There were always neat cars at the shop and the guys who drove them were pretty great, even if they did make fun of me sometimes. But I didn't mind, most of 'em didn't mean it.

I was Virgil's first employee. He didn't pay me when I started but that didn't matter. I knew he would if I just stuck around. My Dad told me that. He said since I wasn't very smart that I had to find a place and just show up every day and keep working and show I was a good worker and sooner or later they'd hire me.

He was drinking when he said that so I wasn't sure if he was jokin or not. I know he loved me but after the accident he was different. Mom said he didn't used to drink so much but I'm not sure if I remember. There's a lot of things I'm not sure I remember, not even the accident. Mom said Dad was drinking that day too.

I remember Dad's truck, a 46 Hudson. There weren't many trucks like it. Dad had the exhaust pipes come out behind the cab like one of those big trucks you see on the highway. He wanted to chrome 'em but he didn't have the money. They'd get real hot when he drove so I wasn't allowed to touch 'em. I did once and it hurt like hell. It burnt the skin on my hand, but I didn't tell nobody. I didn't wanna get in to trouble. I can show ya the scar if ya want?

The accident? It wasn't his fault. He'd been workin on Harold's car, a 38 Plymouth. Harold's car always needed work. Harold brought beer like he always did. They ran out and Dad said he'd run to the store and get more. I jumped in the back of the Hudson and lay down so he couldn't see me. I did that sometimes.

I like ridin in the back of a truck. You can feel the wind hit your face. A couple of the older guys would stand up behind the cab. I wasn't tall enough.

Sometimes I'd sit at the back, leaning against the tailgate. The wind felt good back there. Mom didn't like that. If she saw me she made me sit behind the cab. She said it wasn't safe back there. Dad would just laugh and tell Mom I wasn't a baby.

We took off and Dad was drivin pretty fast. Harold was in the truck too. When I sat up I could see 'em laughin through the back window. Dad had a cigarette in his mouth, a Lucky Strike. That's what the Army gave him in the war.

I leaned against the side of the truck for a while and watched the houses go by. I got somethin in my eye so I decided to move behind the cab when we stopped at a stoplight.

I got up and started to move. Suddenly Dad hit the gas, the truck jumped as he turned.

I know I lost my balance and I remember reachin out and grabbin for the exhaust pipe. I missed it.

I woke up in a room and there were nurses all around me. My head really hurt. Mom was crying and Dad looked really sad. Then I fell a sleep.

The next time I woke up Mom and Dad were still there and there was a doctor shinin a light in my eyes. My head still hurt. I could hardly see, there was stuff around my eyes. I felt a big bandage that went all around my head.

I fell a sleep again.

This time when I woke up people were talkin to me. I don't remember what they said but they let me go home. Mom told me I fell out of the truck and hit my head on the ground, that's why it hurt so much. I had to keep the bandages on for a while. Mom said they operated on my brain.

When the doctor took the bandages off my head I still looked the same. But my head was flatter on one side. The doctor said he put a metal plate in there to protect my brain. A lota stuff got hurt when I fell. He said I'd get headaches a lot but they'd go away after a while. They did.

For a long time Mom and Dad wouldn't let me play with the other kids. Mom said I was fragile, whatever that meant. Dad just looked sad a lot. That's when he drank more. He never got mean when he drank, just sad. He said my accident was his fault, but it wasn't. I knew that but he still felt bad.

Mostly I had to lie in bed. I wasn't able to do much except play with my army men. I found Dad's car magazines and I used to look at 'em over and over. I never had brothers or sisters or nothin so I'd just stare at the magazines. That's when I decided I wanted to work on hot rods.

When I went back to school some of the kids made fun of me. They said I was stupid. Maybe I am, I don't know. The kids that bothered me most were the ones that tried to hit me in the head. They wanted to see if they could break their hand on the metal plate. The teacher would make 'em stop if she caught 'em.

Sometimes it hurt. Them hittin me. Sometimes the headaches hurt more. I tried not to think about it. I'd just put my head on my desk and close my eyes. My head felt better when I closed my eyes. I think cause it was dark. My head didn't hurt when it was dark.

I didn't do good at school and they kept puttin me back. My friends got to go to the next class but I didn't. They put me in with the dummies, that's what they called us, dummies. Some of the kids weren't dumb, they just didn't like school.

Sometimes the Principal came in and took a boy outta class and we wouldn't see him again. I tried to be good. The Principal never came and got me.

I was growing and I got big, just like Dad. Some of the coaches at school wanted me to play sports, but I couldn't.

'Cause of the plate in my head. My parents wouldn't let me do a lotta things the other kids got to do so I stayed home a lot.

Dad didn't work on his car like he used to. He bought a Ford. I don't know what happened to the Hudson, it wasn't around no more. Mostly Dad just went to work and came home. He did stuff around the house and drank beer.

I had all his car magazines and I read 'em over and over. Like I said, I was gonna build hot rods when I grew up. I'd just sit and look at the car magazines for hours.

Teachers always said I couldn't read good, but they were wrong. I could read the car magazines just fine. That's how I learned about Ed "Big Daddy" Roth and George Barris, guys like that. I learned the difference between Carter Carburetors and Holley's and why you wanted to have headers and a good cam in your car if you wanted it to go fast and sound good too.

I could read just fine, the stuff they wanted me to read in school was boring. I didn't care about those stories. Except for one book I found in the library. It was called, *The Magnificent Jalopy* by a guy named John Tomerlin. I really liked that book.

After a while school wasn't fun anymore so I stopped going. That's when I started hangin out at Virgil's. Guys there were always laughing and drinking beer and working on cars. That's what I wanted to do. I remember my Dad laughing when he use to work on cars so I thought I'd like to do that.

Virgil said if I kept the shop clean he'd show me how to work on cars. I swept the shop every day. Sometimes twice a day. I learned where all the stuff went and I would put tools back in their boxes when guys left them out. Sometimes they weren't finished with 'em and would start yellin at me cause I put their tools away. They'd call me dumb, and stuff like that. It hurt my feelings sometimes, even if they didn't mean it.

Chick would tell 'em to stop makin fun of me. He worked there and he was big so they listened to him. He said I was okay and he'd teach me stuff. I learned how to change a car's oil from him. He also taught me that every tool has its place and you need to keep 'em clean so they would work good when you needed 'em. Chick was my friend.

Sometimes Chick and I would drive to Woodburn to see the drag races. He had a friend who raced there and we'd hang around with him in the pits. That's what they call the place where the racecars are. It's so guys can keep workin on their cars between races. I don't know how it got the name "pits", but that's what they call it. It was really loud.

Once after work we went out to the Speedway where they had races. The best part was at the end when they had a big demolition derby and they smashed up all the cars that lost. I don't know if they do that anymore after races, but it sure looked fun. I heard all those places are gone now.

Chick was the first one who let me drive his car. I didn't have a license but he said that was okay he'd teach me so I could get one. And he did. He would take me to parking lots and show me how to use the clutch and shift all the gears. I tried to be careful cause he had a 53 Chevy, which is a really nice car.

After a while Virgil got gas pumps. He said we could make more money sellin gas and he put me in charge of fillin people's tanks and takin their money. He taught me how to make change too.

I was pumpin gas and changin oil and fixin tires all the time. I could find tiny nails in tires that most of the other guys would miss. You have to really concentrate and look for the bubbles when you put the tire in water. Most of the guys didn't like doin stuff like that. They said it was boring. They wanted to work on the racecars.

Lots of guys want to work on the racecars and the hot rods but they never lasted long. Maybe they didn't like to get dirty. I don't know. Lots of guys came and went. Even Chick left. He got married and his wife wanted him to get a real job like at a car dealer or something. I got to go to his wedding and it was fun. Lots of people were drinkin and dancin. I don't drink but I like watching other people have fun.

A couple weeks later Chick said he was leaving to work at the Chevy dealer. Before he left he took me to the DMV, that's where I did my drivers test. He said anyone who was twenty-two years old should have a license and their own car. I passed with flying colors. Chick said to come down to the Chevy dealer sometime and he'd help me buy a car. I never did. I didn't want to tell him I liked Plymouths better. That mighta hurt his feelings and I didn't wanna do that.

I didn't mind walking but it was fun to have a license.

I finally did get a car. It was a DeSoto and it was a really nice one. I know 'cause I used to work on it. Old man Jenkins would bring it in and have me change the oil. He kept it nice and one day he came in and said his kids wouldn't let him drive it anymore cause he was too old. He asked if I wanted to buy it since I always took good care of it. Virgil helped me make a good deal with him and I bought the car.

I'd still have it today if it hadn't gotten wrecked. Some guy who was drinking ran in to it when I was drivin home. The Insurance Company said the car was totaled so they gave me money. Not very much so I had to walk for a while until I could save more. Lucky I wasn't hurt.

I wish people wouldn't drink and drive. It's stupid.

When you stay busy time goes by fast. I try and stay busy. I still live in the same house but my Mom and Dad are gone. Dad died years ago. I was sad that he died but he wasn't very happy for a long time. It seemed like he didn't want to be around anymore. He got sick one day and stopped going to work. He would sit in front of the house in a chair and watch the people go by. He didn't want to eat and he stopped drinking beer, which was good. But mostly he just sat in his chair.

He told me once he was ready to go. I said I didn't want him to but I don't think he listened. When my Dad made up his mind to do something, he did it. Mom says I'm a lot like him that way.

One day he didn't get out of bed. Some guys came and took him and we had a funeral. It was real nice cause some of his friends came. I saw Harold. He was really old. I think he'd been drinking cause his breath smelled bad.

Mom died a couple years later. She was crossing the street coming home from work and collapsed. The doctor said she had a stroke. I had another funeral but hardly anyone came. Just some people who worked with her. They let me take home a bunch of left over food but I threw most of it out. You can only eat so many sandwiches and cakes.

I miss them both a lot. The house is quiet. I thought about getting a dog or cat or something but that seems like a lotta work.

I miss a lotta the guys who used to work here. Not all of 'em. Sometimes I wonder what Chick is doing and maybe he and I could go to some races or something. But I don't have his number and the Chevy dealer closed a long time ago.

We don't get any racecars or hot rods here anymore.

Now it's just me and Virgil and Billy. That's Virgil's son. Well he's not really his son but Virgil raised him. He married Billy's mother and I forget what you call it if you raise someone and they're your son but you're not really their father.

Billy's a good mechanic though.

Sometimes Virgil and Billy make fun of me and call me stupid and I wish they wouldn't. I know they don't mean it. I can't complain though. It's good to have a job.

Not many people come here anymore. Virgil stopped sellin gas a few years ago. He said it was too expensive to keep the pumps filled. Once that happened I had less to do. I miss talkin to the old customers, even if they were just gettin gas. It was nice to see 'em. I used to clean the windshields too. I always used a cloth cause it does a better job. I know they appreciated it. A clean windshield is important.

Now I just do oil changes and fix tires, Oh yeah, I already said that.

Finally I bought another car. A used Rambler Matador. I know Rambler went out of business a long time ago but I got a good deal on it and it's a pretty good car. It's not as nice as the DeSoto but it runs pretty good and that's important. I wouldn't want it to break down and make me late for work. I don't know what they'd do without me at the shop.

Every morning I get here at six-thirty. We don't open until seven but that gives me time to get my work done before we open. Virgil gets here at six, he just sits in his office, smokes cigarettes, and plays solitaire on his computer. He says he's workin on stuff but I just see him play that game. I don't think he's workin on anything anymore. Virgil's lucky. He lives across the street from the shop so he just walks to work. I worry cause sometimes his balance isn't very good either. He's fallen a couple times too. He says he doesn't want any help and that canes are for sissies but I think he needs one. He's a couple years older than me and he used to drink a lot. But not anymore. I think he's afraid he's going to fall again and that's why he stopped. He only drives once a week and that's to visit a friend on Sundays.

Sundays are the only days we're closed. I wish I had a friend that I could visit on Sundays. I just wash my uniforms and watch TV. If the weather is good I work in the yard. Mom always said it's important to keep the yard looking good. It makes a good impression. Even though we never had much money our yard always looked nice. It doesn't take much to make it look nice. I wish some of my neighbors worked more in their yards.

Virgil's been married a couple times. So has Billy. I never got married.

I don't know why, I guess I never met the right person. Sometimes I think what it would be like to be married and have kids. I know they'd be smarter than me, but that's okay. If I had a son I'd teach him all I know about cars. I could teach a daughter too. That would be fun.

I see some of the families in the neighborhood and I think havin a family would be nice. But I don't worry about it. Well just sometimes when it's late and I'm home by myself. Mom always said I'd find a nice girl. Girl, that's what she called them even when I was in my thirties. I'd say, "Mom they're women now. Not girls." She'd laugh and say, "Well they're girls to me." I'd laugh too.

I miss my Mom.

Every morning before we turn on the lights I have to put out all the stuff we might need for the day. Even though we don't have gas anymore the pumps are still there. We have one of those rubber tubes that dings when cars drive over it to tell us when people are here. I wrap up the tube every night and take it inside so it doesn't get stolen. That happened once when we used to leave it outside. So in the mornings I unroll it and put it around the gas pumps.

We still have windshield wipers and water buckets and squeegees and towels and stuff. We don't use 'em much anymore, but it's still important to put 'em out. Just in case we need it. Even though we don't have gas I want to make sure we're ready. Maybe Virgil will decide one day that we'll have gas again. That would be good.

I worry sometimes about the future. What happens if Virgil has to close the shop? Where will I work? Virgil is getting old and with business being bad sometimes he can't pay me on time. That's okay cause I have some money put away so I can live just fine. He always pays me but sometimes it takes an extra week or somethin. I know he's havin it tough.

But if he has to close the shop I don't know where I'd go. I like my job. I like havin a place to go to every day. It's important just like my Dad said. I don't know what Virgil would do without me. I don't think he remembers how to change oil and I know Billy doesn't like doin it. Billy only likes fixing cars.

I wish more people would bring their cars in for oil changes. I know there are those places that just change oil and they're faster and cheaper but I do a better job. I vacuum and wash all the windows and make sure the windshield wipers are good and all the lights work. I take my time cause I wanna do it right. I want people to think I gave them the best oil change they ever got and tell their friends. I want them to come back.

If I could do oil changes all day I'd be really happy. Even though my knees would probably hurt a lot more than they do now.

And maybe Billy wouldn't bother me so much. He says I don't work enough but he wasn't here when I used to do oil changes, fix people's tires,and pump all the gas. There were some days I'd be so tired when I get home I'd fall a sleep in my uniform, before I went to bed.

Those days were hard. But I miss 'em. Sometimes the days are really long when there's nothin to do. That's probably what it would be like if I didn't work here anymore. People tell me I can retire but then I'd just stay home. What good is that? I still want to have a job.

I hope Virgil doesn't die before me.

THE RED MOON
By Mark A. Nobles

My father turned into the driveway a little too fast, just like he always did. The Studebaker's engine growled and the spring shocks squealed as my mother held her breath and closed her eyes, and my brother and I bounced in the back seat, almost hitting our heads on the roof. It was a Sunday night, March 13, 1946, and we were returning home from church. It was a fine spring evening.

I remember the sermon that evening being especially fiery, even for Preacher Bonds. It had been a hell and brimstone, apocalyptic, God fearing sermon and I had been particularly caught up while mother cried, father slept, and Jim, my younger brother, fidgeted.

Preacher Bonds was as charismatic a Southern Baptist preacher as ever lived. Southern Baptist work from the premise that a good Christian is a scared Christian, and they have plenty of good material from which to work. Few denominations can wring fear from the Bible as well as the Southern Baptists. I know what you're thinking, but I don't count the Catholics.

They've had so many more years of practice that, for them, rule by fear is a centuries old art form.

Anyway, Preacher Bonds stayed pretty much in Revelations that night, and his voice was still ringing in my ears as the Studebaker coughed and died in the driveway, and we piled out into the late dusk of evening.

Jim looked up at the sky and pointed. "Look at the size of the moon tonight," he said. I turned and looked up at the moon as it hung just over our neighbor's roof. "And the color," Jim said. "Look at the color." It was red, blood red.

"And the stars shall fall from the sky," said father as he reached down and scooped Jim up in his burly arms, "and the moon shall turn blood red," he bellowed in his deepest voice. "Isn't that what Preacher Bonds said about the start of the end times?"

Jim's eyes got about as big as the moon.

"Bill," mother said to father in her disapproving voice.

Father paid no heed to mother. "Yes, I believe he did," he said, putting Jim back on the ground. He turned in a way that he didn't have to look at mother, and walked into the house.

Mother put her hand on my shoulder, and softly said, "Go on, into the house with both of you."

I look back at that time and wonder why I didn't notice the change as it was beginning. She was pale, my mother, and try as I might to remember now, I can't recall when the life had gone from her voice, but it was already gone on that night. I was only ten, Jim only six, but looking back I wonder how I could have missed it, not seen it coming. Then, I spend an hour watching my own children at play in their backyard, and I realize children have no yesterdays or tomorrows, only todays.

It isn't until adulthood that we try and string all those days together and look at the whole.

That night, after mother tucked us in, we lay in bed, quiet, but wide awake.

"Bent?" Jim said.

"Yes," I answered.

"Is this it? Is this the end of the world or was Dad kidding?"

"Don't know. Dad reads the paper and says the world has gone crazy and with what Preacher Bonds said about the end times, it could be."

"Have you ever seen the moon red like that?" Jim asked. We couldn't see the moon from our beds, but we could remember what it looked like out by the car and its light came rustling in through the curtains.

"Can't say I ever remember it being red," I said with all the wisdom and experience of my one decade of life.

"What should we do? I can't go to sleep. If this is the end of the world, I don't want to sleep through it."

I knew where Jim was leading the conversation. Three summers ago father had built a treehouse in the Live Oak on the east side of the house. Jim hadn't been allowed to climb it until this spring because he had been too small. It was still a new and secret place for him. We had sneaked out there at night a time or two before, but it was always a gamble because the Live Oak was on our parent's side of the house, just a few yards away from their window, which stayed open to catch the breeze during the spring and summer. We had to be really quiet and being quiet did not come naturally to Jim.

"I don't know, Jim. If this is Judgment Day, it might not be a good idea to be caught someplace where we're not supposed to be."

Jim didn't say anything, but after about twenty minutes my imagination began to run away with me as well. If the world was coming to an end, I kinda wanted to be a witness.

"OK," I said, "let's go out to the treehouse, but…"

"We have to be really quiet," Jim finished my sentence for me. "I know. I'm six, not stupid."

Ours was a two-story, craftsman style house with a wraparound porch that sat on the southwest corner of Race and Karnes streets. Because our house was a corner lot with a bigger yard, all the neighborhood kids came to our house to play. I really enjoyed the big yard until I grew strong enough to push a lawnmower.

All we had to do to get to the treehouse was climb out our window to the first story eave that encircled the house. Our bedroom was at the Southwest corner at the back of the house. Once on the roof, we would crawl down the backyard side, around the corner, and up the Karnes street east side until about three feet from our parent's window, which was on the northeast corner of the house. There was a branch from the Live Oak strong enough and close enough for us to climb out and over into the treehouse. I don't know if I truly believed that night was the end of the world, but I do know I believed that if mother had ever caught us on that ledge it would have been the end of the world for us, or at least for me. Jim, being the younger, might only have been maimed.

As we rounded the corner and started down Karnes street, I was quite surprised to find the light still on in our parent's room. I almost decided to turn back. I thought the better of it because Jim was a few feet ahead of me, and he was afraid of heights. He was totally focused on not falling off the eave. I was afraid to say anything or to grab him suddenly for fear he might cry out. I decided to forge ahead, and we crawled into the treehouse with only one small scare. Once, Jim slipped a bit on the limb and rattled the branches regaining his balance. He was a pretty brave kid and although there was a scream in his eyes, not a sound passed his lips.

The treehouse had a ledge on the Karnes street side that the roof didn't cover, so we stretched out side by side on our backs and looked up through the branches at the stars and waited.

They looked as secure in the heavens as ever and none fell as we watched.

Lying in the stillness I could hear my parent's mumbled voices drifting out through their open window. I could only catch a stray phrase or two every few minutes and for a long time, I didn't even pay attention. But after what must have been at least thirty minutes, I realized they were still up and talking. I began to wonder. It had to have been past midnight and mother and father didn't usually stay up past ten, eleven at the most, even on a Saturday night, let alone a Sunday night.

"Jim," I whispered, "what do you suppose they're talking about this late." Jim didn't say a word and when I turned and looked at him, he was sound asleep. He lay there on his back with his mouth open, inhaling and exhaling the shallow, quick breathes of childhood.

I slowly sat up and peeped over the two by four railing and looked into my parent's window. A thin wind briefly brushed back the curtain and I saw my mother sitting on the bed, holding her hands in her lap. I think she looked scared but that could be a detail that slipped into my memory over the many years since. As I sat there looking over the railing, my father passed back and forth by the window. Sometimes it appeared as if he was carrying things, maybe clothes, but I could not tell for sure.

I could not make out their conversation. I sat and strained to listen and hoped for another small gust of wind to provide a glimpse of their discussion.

Father did most of the talking. Mother only saying a few words now and then. After a while father stopped pacing. I couldn't see him any longer, so I assumed he sat down in the overstuffed chair in the corner, out of sight from the window.

They talked about me and Jim for a long time. Every once in a while I'd hear 'the boys' mentioned or one of our names spoken. Mother kept talking about church and Preacher Bonds but I didn't have to hear father to know how he felt about them. He never was much of a churchgoer.

That night seemed as if it passed in an hour. I sat in the treehouse knowing what was happening in my parent's room was important but not thinking to guess what it might be. My pajamas began to get damp and sticky as the morning dew began to form.

I had fallen asleep, my head resting on my hands on the rail when I was startled to consciousness by the light turning out in my parent's room. I raised up and was momentarily relieved, thinking they had finally gone to bed. I stretched out on my stomach and looked over the side of the treehouse towards Race street. I was going to lie there a few minutes to loosen some of the kinks out of my neck and back. After I was sure mother and father were asleep, I'd wake Jim and we'd crawl back to our own beds.

The sound of our front door opening perked my head back up. I heard the front door close followed by footsteps across our porch and down the walk. A man carrying a suitcase walked east on Race heading towards Karnes. The man crossed Karnes and kept on walking until he disappeared into the orange glow of the rising sun.

> The full moon became like blood, and the stars of the sky fell to the earth as the fig tree sheds its winter fruit when shaken by the gale; the sky vanished like a scroll that is rolled up, and every mountain and island was removed from its place.
>
> Rev. ch.6 12-14

SATURDAY IS MY DAY
By Kelley Baker

never sleep in on Saturdays. That's when I go to work. I been workin with my Dad every Saturday since I was six. I'm almost ten now and I wouldn't miss a Saturday for anything. When I grow up I wanna sell cars just like my Dad.

We sell Fords, Chevys, Dodges and Plymouths. Dad calls it a "pot lot" nothin over eight hundred dollars. Some customers can't even afford that. Dad says they're workin people just tryin to get by. Sometimes Dad'll finance their cars himself. He's real good at figurin out who he can trust even if sometimes he has to go to their houses and get the money.

We get some pretty weird lookin cars sometimes. We had an old Renault that had the engine in the trunk. It didn't run though. Dad sold it to some guy who said he could fix it. There was an old Nash that looked like an upside down bathtub and a 58 Ford with a white hardtop. You pushed a button and the top went in the trunk like a convertible. I never saw nothin like it.

We've had a bunch of Studebakers, mostly Larks. Dad's given Mom a couple of the Larks to drive us around in, but he always sells 'em just when Mom gets used to 'em. Sometimes she gets mad at him.

We've had sports cars too. They're small, not like American cars, and they're all convertibles. The coolest are the Bug Eye Sprites. The front end kinda looks like a praying mantis face with their big headlights. I saw pictures in school when we studied bugs.

We also had a really cool bright yellow 58 Chevy with tri-power. That's three carburetors. It was really fast even if Dad said it had a Mickey Mouse transmission in it. That means it's junk. He wanted to sell it before it fell apart. Every night he locked it up in the garage so nobody could steal it.

This car lot has a garage, not like our old one. The old one was down on Foster Road. The address was 5040 SE Foster Road and that's where he got the name of the car lot from. In the front window somebody had painted 5040 SE Foster Used Cars. So everybody just called it 5040 Used Cars.

Even when we moved to 82nd Avenue, he still kept the name even though the address is 1450 SE 82nd. He doesn't care. He thinks it's a good name and so do I.

I like the new location better but I was just a kid when we were at the other lot. There was less traffic so sales weren't so good. That's what Dad says anyway.

The old office was really small but that was okay 'cause on Saturdays it was just me and him. If the weather was good I'd bring my bike and ride on the side street or over to the gas station next door. Dad didn't like me to get too far outta his sight. Especially if he was with a customer.

One day we got a ton of rain and there was this giant mud puddle in back. I rode my bike through it over and over and my feet got soaked. It started rainin again and Dad told me to come in the office so I wouldn't get sick. He made me take my shoes and socks off. He put my socks on the portable heater so they'd dry faster. I turned on the TV and there was a monster movie on Dimension 8. I think it's better to watch monster movies during the day. That way you don't get scared cause it's still light outside.

I was watchin the movie and Dad was helpin a customer. When he came back inside my socks were burnin up. They weren't on fire or nothin, they were smoking an turnin brown. They got kinda crisp. They smelled bad too. They were too crisp and burnt to wear so Dad walked down the street to the surplus store. They have socks there. He said not to say anything to Mom. It was our secret about the burned up socks.

There was a Shakey's Pizza across the street that we went to a couple times. Not too much cause it cost a lot. Dad would tell Mom to bring my sisters and we'd all go over and eat pizza. It was really dark in there. Kinda like a bar, all dark and stuff with a fireplace.

I've never been in a bar but my friend Ronnie Chrowder's Mom works at one called Swanee's. It's in our neighborhood and when me and Ronnie walk home he always has to stop at the bar to tell his mom we're outta school. There's a door that we knock on and his mom opens it. It's always dark and there's guys in there drinkin. Our neighbor Mr. Jackson is always there drinkin beer.

When we'd go to Shakey's I'd always order a root beer cause they serve it in mugs. I'd tell the waitress "no ice please", that way it looks like beer.

The Speck was the other restaurant we'd go to. It was a big drive-in Kentucky Fried Chicken. You could order from your car and after a while a lady came out with your food. The chicken came in a giant cardboard bucket. You could eat in your car if you wanted but we always took it home.

I was eight when we moved to 82nd Avenue. That was two years ago. I was in school so I didn't get to help. It woulda been fun to ride in all the different cars. I wonder how Dad got the cars up there that didn't run? I keep forgettin to ask.

I like the new lot better. There's a Texaco station right next door. That's where Virgil, Chick and Red work. Virgil owns it and Chick and Red just work there. Red never talks much. Sometimes guys pick on him and call him stupid. Chick tells 'em to knock it off and they do. They're all scared of Chick. I am too 'cause he's tough an he always drinks beer when he's workin. He's nice to me though, showin me stuff he's workin on. Since it's right next door I can walk over there and hang around as long as I tell Dad where I'm goin. I watch them work on racecars and hot rods and stuff.

There isn't a Shakey's Pizza by the new lot but that's okay 'cause across the street is a drive-in called Belle's. It's got a big elephant on the sign. They have burgers and fries and stuff, but the best thing they have is fish and chips. It comes in a box and there's lots of fish and french fries in there. It costs fifty-five cents, which seems like a lotta money but there's a lotta food so it's worth it.

I'm not allowed to cross 82nd by myself. It's too busy and I don't want to get smashed by a car going too fast.

Dad helps me cross 'cause there's no stoplights. We stand in front of the lot and wait until there's no cars and then we run across really fast so we won't get run over. Dad gives me the money and I go up to the window and order our food. I always give him the change, but sometimes he let's me keep it.

He goes back to the lot while I wait for our food, 'cause somebody's gotta be there to help customers. I get our food and wait by the street until Dad sees me. Then he crosses back over and helps me carry our food back.

One time this car full a kids went by and they spit on us. Dad was so mad. They were just lucky they kept driving. I asked why they did that. He said some people have no class.

Sometimes I take some of my french fries and put 'em in my chocolate milkshake. I leave 'em in there for a few minutes and then pull 'em out covered with milkshake. It's like they're frozen and they don't taste so salty. I think they're good that way.

We don't always eat at Belle's. Once a month this man shows up with his ten-year-old son. They wear suits even on a Saturday and they sell chicken dinners for lunch. Dad always buys two. Dad says the man's a minister and the chicken's made at their church. Dad orders the chicken in the morning and the Minister and his son come back with the food at lunchtime. It's good, but not as good as fish and chips.

I asked once if the son can stay and play cause we're the same age, but he can't. I guess 'cause he works with his dad just like me.

Dad says it's important to support their church, even though it's a different church than where we go. Dad never goes to church with us on Sundays. Sundays are his only day off so he stays at home and reads the paper. I don't know why he feels it's important for us to go and he never does.

Sometimes a car gets stolen. I think that's cause there's lotsa poor people on 82nd Avenue. Sometimes the police find 'em and sometimes they don't. Sometimes a car is all smashed up when we get it back and we can't sell it. Then the guy from the junkyard takes it.

I've been to the junkyard a bunch of times. It's full of smashed cars. We get parts there for some of our cars that need to get fixed. Dad says the parts are just as good as new and they don't cost so much. I get to go out in the junkyard and walk around. There's cars all stacked on top of each other, or they're just layin there with their guts taken out.

They have cars that were in bad wrecks. I was lookin around to see if maybe I could see some blood where people got hurt, but I didn't see any. Maybe they cleaned off the blood before it got taken to the junkyard?

One time Dad hired Uncle Dave to work for him. Uncle Dave is Dad's brother but they aren't alike at all. Uncle Dave smokes cigarettes and is pretty fat. Dad says Uncle Dave is lazy but he needed a job so Dad helped him.

Uncle Dave didn't last long sellin cars. I'm not sure if he even sold one. Most of the time he just ordered fish and chips at Belle's. Uncle Dave found a bunch of firecrackers in Dad's desk. I knew they were in there too and I asked Dad if we could light 'em. He said we were waitin for Fourth of July and then we would. Uncle Dave didn't wanna wait. He would smoke his cigarettes and light the firecrackers in the office. They would echo off the walls really loud. I thought that was cool. Dad didn't.

One day Uncle Dave didn't come to work. Dad said he got a job drivin a taxi. He said that was a better job for Uncle Dave, sittin on his butt all day drivin around and talkin. He never comes to the lot anymore.

Other guys would work for Dad too sometimes, but they never lasted long. One guy was named Harold. Dad said he was a painter but I never found out if he meant pictures or houses. Harold liked to drink beer, a lot. Somebody told Dad that Harold had a bad temper but he was always nice to me. He stopped workin for Dad when he got arrested. I don't know the whole story but I heard Dad tell somebody that Harold was drunk and when he came home his best friend was in bed with his girlfriend. So Harold killed 'em both.

I don't think that was a good thing to do. I mean his best friend must not have been a nice guy if he did that. And why would you want a best friend like that anyway? Ronnie Chrowder makes me mad sometimes but I wouldn't beat him up or anything, we're best friends.

I think Harold's probably in prison.

There's always stuff to do at a car lot. In the morning Dad gives me this giant metal ring that has a lotta smaller key rings on it for the cars on the lot. It's my job to put all the keys in the cars.

You have to do it in order cause the keys are on the ring in order. I always start at the front of the lot and put the keys in the cars that are closest to the street. I don't have to put keys in the cars at the back of the lot cause most of 'em don't run.

After that I go around and start some of the cars to make sure they still run. I only start the automatics 'cause I'm not tall enough to start the cars with clutches. You have to push in the clutch, then you can start it. If you don't push in the clutch the car will jump and that's bad. So I can't start the cars with clutches until I'm taller.

I don't like startin Fords. You put the key in on the left side of the steering wheel. It's hard to reach around the left side to turn the key while you use your right foot to pump the gas. I can do it all right, but it's hard. I'm kinda stretched out. I like the other cars cause their keys are on the right side.

I'd never buy a Ford.

It can be pretty embarrassing to try and sell somebody a car that won't start. It might have a dead battery or is outta gas or somethin is broken. If a car won't start I tell Dad. He goes out and tries to start it and if it won't start for him he'll tell Dutch about it.

Dutch is a mechanic who sometimes works for Dad. I don't know why they call him Dutch cause that's not his real name. I mean who would call their kid Dutch? Dad says it's 'cause he's from the old country. I don't know what country that is. I don't think we've studied it in school yet.

Dutch works on the railroad at night and only comes in when Dad needs him to fix a car. He wears striped overalls that always get dirty when he works. He's really big and his hands are always dirty too.

It's important for the cars to be clean when people first look at 'em. If a car is clean it means it's been kept up good. So on Saturdays I wash cars. Dad pays me ten cents a car and let me tell you it's hard work. I pull the hose out of the back and fill up a big bucket with soap. Not like soap you have at home, this is special car washin soap. It comes in a big can and it's powdery. I dump a cup full of powder in the bucket then I spray water on it. I like sprayin the powder cause it makes it get all bubbly. Dad says I'm wastin soap, but he lets me do it anyway.

We have this thing that looks like a mop with all this stringy stuff hangin off it. You put your hand inside and use it like a giant sponge. I can't really reach the tops of the cars. Some of the cars are really big, like Chrysler's and Nash's an stuff.

I stand on the bumpers to reach the backs of the hood and trunk but sometimes the bumper is all wet and slippery. I almost fell off a couple times.

Some afternoons Dad gives me money and I walk two car lots over where they have a Coke machine. I buy us two bottles of Coke. Actually I get a grape soda for me. It tastes better. When I have my bike Dad lets me ride to the little store that's a couple blocks away. I have to ride through three small car lots and then through Buxton Motors, the big Rambler lot. They all know me so sometimes they wave.

I ride down to 81st and then go two blocks and there's the little store.

One time when I went there an older kid asked me if I'd put this thing under a car's tire that was sitting in front of the store. It was two pieces of metal and in the middle it had a buncha rolls of caps. The kind we put in our cap guns to make 'em sound like we were really shootin. It was like a cap sandwich. He said if the car ran over it, it would make a big explosion when all the caps popped at once. I told him politely that I didn't want to do that.

The man who owned the car was standin right there and he told the boy he could put it under the tire and he'd drive over it but if it did any damage the boy would have to pay for it.

I didn't want to get in the middle of that cause the man was pretty big, and I couldn't tell if he was jokin or not. I went in and got a bag of peanuts for Dad and a Payday for me. I went real slow gettin my bike so I could hang around to see if the boy would do it. I kinda wanted to see the explosion. But not if it was gonna be too big.

I never heard anything so I bet the kid chickened out.

You would think that being at a car lot would be all work and no play but it isn't. One time I brought my basketball with me and I was dribbling it all over the place. I found an old empty oil drum so I decided to use it for a basket. It was in the garage where Dutch worked on cars so it had lots of grease on it. But I didn't care it made a pretty good basket.

Dad was afraid I'd miss the drum when I was shootin and the ball 'd go out in the street, so he made me play behind the office. That way if I missed the basket the ball would hit the wall and stop.

The only problem was when the ball went inside the drum, cause I'd have to reach inside to get it. It was pretty deep so I had to bend way over. After I was playing for a while I saw that my shirt had a big ol' stain on it from the drum. It was really black from all the grease and stuff.

I thought Mom would be mad cause it was a pretty new shirt. Not real new, but pretty new. It was also my favorite. It was a surfer shirt, ya know with big black and white stripes on it. The kind of shirt surfers wear. I want to be a surfer but we didn't live near the beach so I just wear the shirt.

Anyway, the big stain was on one of the white stripes. Figures, right? If it had been on a black stripe probably no one woulda saw it. When I went home Mom was not happy. She said she'd try to fix it but it was a good shirt and I shouldn't have worn it out to the lot if I was gonna get it dirty.

She had to use bleach to get the grease out. It worked pretty good cause I didn't see any stain on it. But the bleach turned the black stripes brown. It didn't look very cool with the brown stripes, so I don't wear it anymore. Who ever heard of a brown and white surfer shirt?

The coolest thing though is when it's time to go home Dad lets me pick which car we drive. Sometimes he says "No" if I pick a car that doesn't have much gas in it. He never likes to put gas in the cars cause what happens if you fill a car up with gas and somebody buys it? Then you lost all that money that you spent on gas.

Dad got a motorcycle once and I wanted to ride that home. It was a white Honda 300 Dream. That's what it was called, a "300 Dream". This was before there was laws about helmets and stuff. Dad said okay cause it was summer and the weather was good. We drove down Front Avenue. That's the way Dad liked to go 'cause there was never a lot of traffic 'cause that's where all the train tracks are. Sometimes we'd get stuck behind a train and have to wait, which was okay when we had peanuts to eat.

We were going pretty fast when we hit one of the train tracks and the motorcycle flew up in the air. We were flying off the ground, which was pretty neat. But as we started to come back down the motorcycle felt like it was tipping over. I was pretty scared for a second 'cause I didn't want to wipe out on the street, but Dad was able to straighten it out so that when we landed we were tipped over just a little and then the motorcycle was straight again. I don't think Dad was scared but when we got to the next railroad tracks he went slower so we didn't fly.

Mom was mad when she found out that we rode the motorcycle all the way home. We never did that again.

Havin a car lot is pretty neat 'cause you get to drive all sorts of different cars home. On the days I have to go to school, I get up early to see what Dad drove home. There's always a different car in our driveway. Mom doesn't like that. She says the neighbors always look at us like they don't know if we're comin or goin. I'm not sure what that means but I think Mom just wants to have the same car all the time. I'm glad we don't.

It'd be great to go to the lot every day after I'm done with school and work with Dad all the time. I think he'd like that too.

A NIGHT IN ROBERT LEE
By Mark A. Nobles

"Roxanne" blared from the speakers as the black, '79 T-Bird rolled west down State Highway 158. The big bird's taillights shone towards Bronte and the headlights would soon cast illumination on Robert Lee, Texas, population 1,202, God fearing, mostly Baptist, souls.

Dead soldiers that once held Milwaukee's Beast rattled and rolled in the rear passenger floorboard completely out of rhythm and tune with The Police. The sun was well down and the T-Bird's fuel gauge was nearing empty.

"You gotta get laid, or go to the circus, man," said Bill. "You got the funk and need to do something to shake it."

"Every woman I meet has her legs crossed and the circus ain't in town," said Ray. "I'm starting to think I don't have the funk, I think I am the funk."

"Be the funk."

"Fuck the funk."

The T-Bird barreled past the city limit sign of Robert Lee. "We need gas," said Ray.

"And smokes," Bill belched, "and beer. And chips, or jerky, something to eat, I got the munchies."

"Think this rinky-dink has a gas station?"

"Hell, I'm just prayin' it ain't a dry county," said Bill. Spotting a gas pump in the distance he continued, "Over there, over there, over there!"

"Shit, man, I see it," said Ray.

"Then act like it and slow the fuck down."

Ray cut sharply into the gravel parking lot of the Quick-N-Git gas and convenience store. Ray looked around and could see no brand for the gas but the price was dirt cheap compared to Fort Worth and they weren't getting much farther down the road with the needle past E and the T-Bird guzzling at eleven miles to the gallon.

Ray was a taut mass of high dense muscle and high-tension nerves. At 5' 6" people said he had a bad case of little man's complex, but those that knew him understood he was just wound too tight and would still have been a quick tempered asshole at 6' 5."

Ray pulled the T-Bird up to the pumps and slid to a stop, pitching gravel and kicking dust. Turning to Bill he said, "Pitch in, man, you know the deal, no ass, no gas, no ride." He held out his right hand, palm up.

Bill shivered, "It creeps me out when you say things like that, dude." He pulled out his wallet, dug around for a five-dollar bill and handed it to Ray. "Get some Pearl if they got it."

"Pearl," Ray said disgustedly.

"It's good, and it's cheap."

"It's cheap," said Ray as he took the fiver, opened the car door and stepped out. "Start pumping, I'll pay." He walked around the front of the T-Bird and headed into the convenience store. Bill opened the passenger door and walked around the rear of the car to begin pumping gas.

Ray walked in to the Quick-N-Git and immediately noticed the girl behind the counter. She was tall, fit, and tan. Her hair, shoulder length and honey brown. Her eyes were lightning blue and gray. Everything about her was like a smile. Her eyes smiled, her posture smiled, her movement smiled like a child at play, even her aura smiled in contentment and innocence. Ray's head swiveled to keep her in sight as he headed to the beverage coolers in the back. It wasn't until he reached the beer section that he pried his eyes off the girl. Perusing the selection, he spotted the Pearl in the cooler, opened the glass door, and reached right over the good but cheap beer to grab two sixers of Bud. With beer in hand, Ray's head swiveled back to the counter to gaze again at the girl. As he approached to pay for the beer and gas, he walked straighter and taller than his normal Doonesbury cool slouch.

"Hello," said the girl as Ray sat the two six packs on the counter.

"Evening," said Ray as he reached for a handful of jerky sitting in a box by the register.

"Are you in the Thunderbird?" she asked, darting her lightning eyes out the front where Bill was now replacing the nozzle on the pump.

"Indeed, I am," said Ray.

"It don't look like he's coming in," she said.

Ray smiled at the girl because he didn't know what else to do.

The girl smiled back but a trace of bewilderment flashed across her face. "I don't know how much gas he pumped," she said.

Broken from his trance, Ray half blurted, "Oh, yeah, right," he looked out the window at Bill, now seated in the passenger seat. Ray cocked his head in Bill's direction, "He must of forgot," said Ray. He began to walk to the door but kept his eyes on the girl. "He ain't too bright," Ray threw a manly giggle at the end of the sentence. The girl returned the smile, this greatly pleased Ray. Reaching the door, Ray opened it, leaned out and shouted to Bill, "How much did it take!"

Startled, Bill flinched. He turned and shouted back, "You said put in ten, so I put in ten."

Ray shrugged his shoulders, waved his arms, bent at the elbows, palms up, and mouthed 'what?'

"Ten dollars," Bill repeated, stretching out the word dollars for emphasis.

Ray shook his head and returned to the counter. The girl was punching buttons on the register. "Ten on the gas," said Ray.

"I heard," said the girl. "I rung it up and I got the beer and jerky."

"Thank you."

"Anything else?"

"I couldn't find the corn chips."

"Huh. They should be with the potato chips," she furrowed her brow, walked from behind the counter and down the middle of the three isles in the store. Ray watched her walk.

Reaching the section with all the chips, she stooped, grab a bag of corn chips and stood straight as a 2x4. "They're right here, silly," she held the bag towards Ray. "Do you want them?

"Yes," said Ray. "I want them very much."

She walked back to the counter and rung up the chips. "I love Eric Clapton," she said as she bagged Ray's purchases.

Ray looked down at his shirt, it was an Eric Clapton concert tee he had bought a scant month before after seeing him perform at the Tarrant County Convention Center. "Yeah, he's great,"

Ray stammered. He had found his conversation starter with the girl. He was pleased.

"Are you in the band?" she asked.

Ray was stunned and confused. Was she yanking his chain? Was this a test? Why would she assume he was in Eric Clapton's band just because he was wearing a concert tee, for Jiminy's sake? This was not the conversation starter he was prepared for. He was going to talk about going to concerts, not playing on a worldwide tour with Eric freaking Clapton. But then he looked up from his chest and into her eyes. Pure innocence and smile.

"I'm not in the band," he heard himself saying. "I'm a roadie and guitar tech."

"I know what a roadie is but what is a guitar tech?" she said with great interest.

"I work on and tune Eric's guitars before every show." Words were just coming out of Ray's mouth without any engagement with his brain. A smile from a beautiful girl will shut down a boy's brain completely but have no such effect on his mouth or other bodily functions such as erratic breathing, rapid heartbeat, and, well, blood flow to other appendages.

"Wow," she said. The admiration and wonder in her voice sounded to Ray like a chorus of angels singing hymns in heaven. "So you make Eric Clapton sound great."

"Well," Ray tore his eyes away from the girl and looked down at his feet. His brain briefly flickered to life. "Not really, there are three other guitar techs, I'm pretty new, so, I mostly only work on the guitars Eric doesn't play much."

"Wow, that is so cool," she said. She looked Ray straight in the eyes, making him feel warm and content. "Where ya'll headed?"

"Arizona," replied Ray. He began to panic because he could not remember if the tour dates were printed on the back of his shirt. He did not know if Clapton's Backless Tour headed east or west after leaving Fort Worth. "I'm from Fort Worth and after the show there, I stayed a while to visit family. You know, being on the road is lonely, so I wanted to reconnect."

"Ahh, that's sweet," she said. "It gives me hope out here in the middle of nothin' that a Texas boy can go off and live a rock star life."

"Oh," Ray said self modestly, "I'm not a rock star, I just work with one, ah, what's your name?"

"Deedee," she said, pointing to her name tag pinned just above her right breast. Ray glanced at the tag but quickly looked back into her eyes.

"What do the double D's stand for? As if I didn't know." Ray winked when he said double D's. It was his lame attempt at naughty, sexual innuendo.

Deedee's eyes widened, "You know what my D's stand for?" she said.

I, uh, well, I was, I mean, no, I don't."

"Are you teasing me?" she said. "Well, I'll tell you, Deedee stands for Daphnee, with two e's, Dorlene. Daphnee Dorlene is both my granma and my great granma's name. Momma don't rightly remember, but maybe even my great-great granma."

"But it's not your momma's name?"

"No, her name is Sally."

"Well, Daphnee Dorlene is a lovely name and so is Sally. I'm sure your mother, grandmother, and great grandmother were all lovely and kind women if they all led to producing such a beautiful woman as you." Ray was on a roll and laying it thick.

Awww, thank yewww," Deedee said, blushing a little. In west Texas, really, anywhere in Texas, the one-syllable word 'you' is often stretched in length, well beyond any post-grad, six-syllable word. It is enunciated until all breath is drained from the speaker's lungs.

"I don't suppose you and your friend have any reason to hang out for a bit in Robert Lee or any parts about," said Deedee. As she spoke she swung her upper body to and fro and looked at Ray with those eyes, those amazing, smiling eyes.

"Not really, but we're in no hurry, either," Ray said. His heart was pounding through his chest, as he believed he was about to be invited to stick around.

"My friend Buster's daddy has a ranch out a ways on Ranch Road 2034. We have beer busts out there," said Deedee. The more nervous she became the faster her torso twisted. "It's not the kinda parties you're used to, I know, but they're fun and it's pretty out there at night, with the stars and all."

"Sounds, cool," said Ray. Score! Is what he was thinking.

"Really!"

"Sure."

"The turn off is kinda hard to find if you don't know where you're going," if possible, Deedee's eyes and entire countenance brightened and smiled even more. "I get off work at eight, if ya'll want, you can come back and meet me here in the parking lot and follow me out there."

"Sounds like a plan, Deedee." Ray was grinning from ear to ear. "Do I need to buy more beer?"

"Oh, shoot, no. Buster's dad keeps plenty of beer in the barn, he's got a fridge and all, out there. It's Pearl but it don't cost nothin' and he don't mind us drinkin' it."

Ray shuffled his feet and drew a deep breath, "And, well, you don't have a boyfriend that might take insult to me being there, do you?"

"Aww, no, I've grown up with all the boys around here since we were babies. They're more like brothers to me." Ray was willing to bet his bottom dollar that the boys in Coke County did not think of Deedee as a sister.

"Great," said Ray. "I don't need an ass kicking on a Saturday night in Robert Lee."

Deedee blushed and waved Ray off. "Get out of here. Now you're just fooling with me."

"Alright, I'm out of here," said Ray as he picked up his beer, corn chips, and jerky off the counter. "See you at eight."

"Bye!" said Deedee.

Ray left the Quick-N-Git, walked to the T-Bird, opened the back driver's side door, put the sixers in the cooler, tossed the bag of corn chips and jerky in the general direction of Bill, closed the rear door, opened the front, and jumped behind the wheel.

"That took forever," Bill said as he dug in the bag, examining the contents.

"I was talking to a girl," said Ray.

"Sweet! Did you get her number? Does she have a friend? Did you find a party for us out here in no man's land?" Bill liked to conjecture.

"No," said Ray flatly.

Ray started the T-Bird, threw it into drive, and peeled out of the parking lot. He pointed the big, black bird east towards Fort Worth.

✦✦✦✦✦

At the time, Ray did not consciously know why it was best to head home and not accompany Deedee to Buster's daddy's ranch. As the years piled up, however, he was glad he did not attend the beer bust.

Life will kick you in the ass sometimes and over the next forty odd years, Ray had his fair share of ass whoopin's. Two divorces, a child lost to drug and alcohol addiction, and three failed businesses. Each tragedy set Ray to thinking about his life and the choices he made. He never regretted not going to the party at the ranch and possibly sleeping with Deedee. She was and continued to be the most beautiful woman he had ever seen, but he didn't feel he missed out, not having sex with her. He had plenty of sex over the years and had given and received plenty of love.

When marriages and relationships failed Ray, when businesses went belly up, when happiness and contentment seemed to Ray like a carrot on a stick, always beyond his feeble grasp, he took comfort in the knowledge that somewhere, out in west Texas, there was a beautiful, kind woman, telling her grandkids about the time Eric Clapton's guitar tech pulled through the Quick-N-Git in Robert Lee and flirted with her.

To someone, Ray is and always would be a rock star.

INCIDENT AT ARRAH WANNA
By Kelley Baker

Do you go to Hell if you lie to a pastor?

He's not a real pastor; he's the youth pastor. Does that count? I know I shouldn't lie but all the youth leaders say I'm going to Hell anyway. Except Pastor Charlie, he never tells me that.

Pastor Charlie looked right at me and asked if I had any involvement. I looked right back at him and said, "No sir."

He forced me into it. He asked me point blank, in front of other people. He put me in a bad position.

I wasn't the one who got sick and threw up in the prayer meeting. And I wouldn't rat out my friends.

If he hadn't asked me I wouldn't have lied.

But he did, and I did.

It all started when I found out our youth group was going to Camp Arrah Wanna for a weekend retreat, in the snow. I'm thinking snowball fights, hiking, and getting away from my parents for the weekend.

1970 started off as a pretty good year. I started high school and smoked pot for the first time.

I still go to the Baptist Church even though I don't really believe anymore.

We're American Baptists and that's different from Southern Baptists or Conservative Baptists. Those people can't dance or drink or smoke, although I'm sure they all do when no one's looking. We can do all of that stuff but I think we have to be careful about the drinking.

I'm not a bad kid. Although most of the parents and some kids at church would disagree. Betsy's parents hate me and always say that I'm going straight to Hell. But I look at their sons with their white shirts, ties, and crew cuts and tell myself if they're all going to Heaven then I'll take Hell.

One time the youth leaders organized a trip to see *The Cross and The Switchblade*, that movie with Pat Boone. I didn't go because it sounded stupid. Later, Betsy's Dad told me that of all the kids at church I was the one who really needed to see that movie.

Betsy's Dad looks like a ferret without all the hair. When he says stuff to me I try not to laugh thinking about his ferret face. Sometimes it's hard not to.

This is a hard time for me. The world is changing but everyone still treats me like a kid. I'm almost fifteen. I wanted to be at Woodstock so bad, but I was only thirteen and there was no way my parents would let me travel cross-country by myself for something like that. If there's another Woodstock when I'm eighteen I'm going.

My buddy Carl and I talk about this a lot. We're the only ones who listen to music that the youth leaders don't approve of.

He discovered Jethro Tull and Steppenwolf; I turned him on to The Who and The Kinks.

The weekend was going to be great. Carl and I were going to have a blast. I scored two joints, and he got some hash.

I've never smoked hash before but I've heard about it. That's the stuff they smoke in India. I think they have visions on it too. Maybe that's peyote. I'm not sure. Carl's a lot smarter than me. He's always discovering stuff that I didn't know about. Anyway I was really looking forward to smoking hash.

Camp Arrah Wanna is on Mt Hood. It's a big Baptist camp that mostly gets used in the summer. Carl and I have been going to camp since we were ten. You do lots of hiking, swimming, and Christian stuff. You live in small cabins, 7 to a cabin, and a counselor.

One year, Carl and I had a really old counselor named Cal who drove an ancient Rambler. He was the pastor at a church in Milton-Freewater, Oregon. He was okay even if he did smear peanut butter all over his scrambled eggs. There was another old guy in a different cabin who asked all the guys every night whether they had a "BM" that day. If you said, "No." he made you go down to the bathrooms and go until you did. That guy was weird.

The little cabins don't have any heat so in the winter they open this big building where everyone sleeps in two dorms. One for boys and one for girls.

When we got to camp, there was snow everywhere! It must have been a couple feet deep.

We put our stuff in the dorm and staked out our beds. Halfway down the row as far from the two counselors as we could get. They sleep at each end and the last thing you want is to have your bed close to them. They're always telling you to be quiet and go to sleep.

One of the counselors is Pastor Charlie. Even though he's the youth pastor he's an okay guy. I think he's still in pastor school or whatever you call it. His sister is our age so even though he's a pastor he's pretty young. You can talk to him.

The plan was for Carl and I to ditch everybody. We knew the only way not to get caught was to stay low-key.

After the morning prayers and meetings there were a couple hours where nothing was planned. I kept watch while Carl got out the hash. Then I dug through my suitcase and got the two joints.

I forgot matches. Luckily Carl had a Zippo lighter with some weird little crest on it. I'm not sure where he got it but it was pretty fancy looking. Carl always has stuff like that.

We took off out the back door and made for the woods. About a half-mile through the snow were some old deserted cabins. They were falling apart and even during the day they looked haunted. I always think of those stories about the guy with hooks for hands that preys on teenagers.

As we took off John Johnson spotted us. John's a jock but he's okay.

We pretended not to hear John and kept walking. Which was really hard as the snow came up to our knees. He followed us anyway. Being a jock he's in better shape than we are and it didn't take him long to catch up.

"Where you goin?"

"Just walkin…"

"Can I come a long?"

I wanted to say "No." But Carl just shrugged. We'd deal with it later.

The three of us trudged along in silence until we got to the cabins.

They were just like I remembered. The doors had been pulled off and God knows what kinds of animals were living in there.

Carl and I headed toward the cabin in the back. We figured this would be the one with the least amount of traffic if any of our "church couples" wanted to tempt the guy with the hooks for hands.

The cabin was up a small hill and in the deep snow it was a lot harder to get to. Finally, we staggered inside. It wasn't as dark as I thought it'd be. The boards on the walls had huge spaces between them letting in the reflected light from the snow. Most of the floorboards looked okay, but we could see holes in the floor where others had thought they were okay too.

I pulled out a joint. They weren't the best looking joints, but they were okay. I bought them from an older girl at high school. She was a sophomore and kind of a hippie. At fifty cents each it was all my lunch money. She even rolled them for me because I didn't know how.

Carl pulled out the Zippo and lit me up.

"What's that?" John asked.

I passed the joint to Carl and he inhaled.

"Is that Marijuana?"

Carl nodded.

"You want to try it?" I asked.

John shook his head.

"I'm gonna take off."

"You're not gonna say anything are you?" Carl asked.

John shook his head again.

We knew he wouldn't. He may be a jock, but he wasn't a snitch.

As he turned to leave we heard a bunch of noise.

Another group of guys was heading our way. It was Phil, Kevin, his little brother Scott, and some guy we didn't know. They all lived way past the suburbs where there were still farms.

They busted into our little cabin.

"What's goin on?" Phil asked.

Carl and I shrugged. John left. We probably should have gone with him.

"You guys interested in a drink?" Kevin asked.

"We got a bottle and a few beers." Scott said as he pulled two cans of beer out of his coat pockets.

Kevin and the other guy pulled out a couple beers each. Phil had a bottle of whiskey.

"Do you guys drink?" said the guy we didn't know.

"Yeah, we drink. But we came out here to smoke." I said as I pulled the half smoked joint out from behind my back. "Do you guys smoke?"

"Yeah, we smoke." Kevin shot back. He knew what I was implying and he wasn't having any of it.

"But do you smoke hash?" Carl said as he pulled out his pipe.

This hash pipe was a thing of beauty. Carl made it himself. It was an old cardboard toilet paper roll that he covered in tin foil. There was a hole cut into it and a little screen in the hole. You placed the hash on the screen, covered one end of the toilet paper roll with your hand and the other with your mouth and then you inhaled for all you were worth as someone else lit the hash.

An engineering marvel. No fancy pipe to lose, or get found by your parents. I told you Carl was smart.

After a few hits of the hash I was feeling great. I had a drink or two from the whiskey to show I wasn't a wuss. I was smart enough to know that you don't drink fast and you're careful what you mix.

After a while we took off, leaving those other guys behind as they kept drinking. We wandered around the woods in the snow. It was really cool and quiet, except the crunching of our boots.

We headed back to the lodge knowing there were other things going on and we didn't want to be gone too long.

It was about an hour later when the whole group got together. There was some singing, some prayers, some preaching, and some vomit.

Vomit?

In the middle of Pastor Charlie's sermon I heard it. That low growl when everything in your stomach decides it wants out, and it gets it's wish.

I looked down the row of chairs and there at the far end Kevin's friend was blowing chunks all over the floor. And it reeked of alcohol!

He is so busted was my first thought. We are so busted was my next thought.

Who is that kid anyway? I know Kevin and his brother are cooked, probably Phil too. There's nothing linking Carl and I to this, but Betsy's parents will try.

The counselors took him into the dorm. Kevin and Scott followed behind.

Pastor Charlie said, "Let's all take a break and meet back here in half an hour."

The other kids were all talking as Carl and I looked at each other. Had we stashed the rest of our stuff well? No way we could go into the dorm and find out 'cause that's where they took the vomiting guy.

Carl and I laid low and avoided talking to anyone. We stood off to one side, but I could see Betsy's Mom was eyeing us.

Two guys who worked there came in with a big bucket of sawdust. They poured the sawdust all over the puke and then swept it all up and put it back in the bucket. It looked disgusting but it didn't smell anymore.

The half hour went by quickly and Pastor Charlie called everyone back.

"It seems as though a few people brought some alcohol on this trip and have ruined the weekend for everyone else. I think we should break off into small groups and discuss this and maybe we can decide as a group what the punishment should be..."

I looked at Carl. Did that no-name son of a bitch name names? Or was it Kevin? We knew Kevin well enough he wouldn't talk. He'd say it was his fault. We weren't sure what his brother would say. Did no-name kid even know our names?

We were divided into small groups. Carl and I were separated. Not a problem, neither of us would break. And we certainly wouldn't give up the other.

Pastor Charlie was leading my group.

First there was a lecture about alcohol and how the behavior of a few had ruined the weekend for everyone. Then it came.

"What do you all think we should do with the people who are involved?" Pastor Charlie asked.

One kid said their parents should be called and come up to the mountain and pick them up. Others were agreeing and saying they should have to get up in front of the group and apologize.

I kept quiet. I knew if parents were called that would be bad. This would be one of those lessons and soon everyone in the church would know about it. I was lost in thought when I realized everyone was staring at me.

I blinked. Pastor Charlie was talking to me.

"Harold, you've been awful quiet. What do you think should happen?"

I mumbled something and shrugged my shoulders.

That's when Pastor Charlie looked straight at me and said those horrible words…

"Did you have any involvement in this?"

I was trapped. What could I say? "I didn't really drink with them. I was smoking pot."

Then I thought, could he smell it on me like they say you can smell fear? Did I smell of pot? Or hash? Were my eyes red? Was I getting paranoid? Did I look like a deer in headlights?

"No sir."

Pastor Charlie looked at me for quite a while. I'm not sure if he was buying it or not. His gaze shot right through me. I just sat there looking back at him, trying not to blink or look guilty.

Finally he turned to the rest of the group and started talking again. I felt relieved. I can't remember what our group decided, but soon enough it was time to go back in to the big hall.

I sat next to Carl. We didn't speak but I knew he hadn't cracked. I looked to my left and saw Kevin, Scott and Phil. They were all staring straight ahead. I figured Kevin and Scott's parents would probably beat the hell out of them. They seemed like that type.

Pastor Charlie started talking about "the incident". He and the counselors had talked among themselves and I couldn't tell if they had come up with a plan or not.

No-name kid appeared from the boy's dorm. He walked unsteadily up front with one of the counselors helping him and apologized to the whole group.

He'd better apologize. Apologize for not being able to hold his liquor. What a wuss.

Pastor Charlie looked out at us and asked if anyone else had anything to say.

Kevin got up, walked to the front and apologized. His brother followed him.

Then the damnedest thing I ever saw. This other kid Rick got up, went to the front and HE APOLOGIZED!

What the Hell? He wasn't even there.

Rick's thinks he's so cool and all the girls think he's so cute cause he tries to play guitar and he loves all the attention from the girls. I've known him since kindergarten and I never liked him. He wasn't a drinker. He certainly wasn't a smoker! And he certainly hadn't been there!

Why was he doing this?

Then I saw it. Some of the girls were crying, but I could see that they were thinking he was even cooler. They thought he was one of the "bad boys!"

Rick was "confessing" and apologizing with tears streaming down his face. Unbelievable. Phil was still seated, stone faced. He wasn't getting up. He was going to let the other guys take the fall.

Then I saw John. He was looking right at me. I knew John would never rat us out, and he hadn't. But he was looking at me like he was waiting for me to do something.

Now I'm not sure what possessed me but suddenly I found myself getting up and heading to the front of the room. There was no way I was going to let Momma's Boy Rick confess to something he wasn't part of just to be cool.

I got up front and said something to the group, maybe I apologized, maybe I didn't, I don't remember. But I stared down Rick. He knew that I knew he wasn't there.

I saw the counselors looking at each other and nodding as I spoke. I'm sure they were just confirming to themselves that all of this was my fault.

Carl followed me up there. He didn't have to, but he did.

All those other guys were staring at their shoes, but Carl and I were looking straight out at all those faces. We knew what the counselors thought and at that moment I'm not sure if we were defiant, or still stoned. But I knew that both of us would take whatever punishment was dished out without a word, or tears.

The whole room got quiet. Then I realized, the counselors had a huge problem on their hands.

This incident didn't involve one or two bad apples. There were six of us up there. Now our youth group isn't that big, so six bad apples is a lot. And if so many of us had been involved didn't that reflect badly on the youth leaders? A weekend retreat turned into a "beer bust" and the counselors and youth leaders let it happen?

We'd get a lot of crap for our involvement, but the adult counselors would be looked at even worse.

All of a sudden I knew there was no way parents would be called. It was too risky for the counselors and poor Pastor Charlie. He was the Youth Minister for Christ's sake!

Pastor Charlie and the rest of the adult counselors must have realized this because they got together really quickly for a conference. We still had to stand in front of the group while this was going on.

When Pastor Charlie finally came back up front it had been decided. No parents would be called. This would be settled among the whole group.

Prayers were said. There was more apologizing (not by either Carl or myself) and forgiveness handed out. Finally it was decided that we would all go outside and have a giant snowball fight.

The snowball fight was supposed to take out all our aggressions and I suppose our transgressions as well.

The amazing part was that throughout all of this Phil just sat there looking stone faced. He never copped to anything.

Pastor Charlie found me later.

"You lied to me." He said.

"You left me no choice, asking me in front of everyone."

Pastor Charlie thought about it for a minute. He nodded and walked away.

The whole thing blew over pretty quickly. It helped that the next weekend the high school group went up there and they got busted … for alcohol and pot. This time parents were called.

Pastor Charlie wasn't involved with that trip which I was glad about. Those youth group leaders were the subject of a lot of gossip around the church. Most of them quit.

I spent the next six months smoking a lot of pot with the head Pastor's kid, Tony. We would sneak out during his Dad's sermons, smoke, and then go to a nearby café and drink coffee.

One night in youth group some choir from another church was supposed to come and visit us. Betsy's Dad told us that Satan had given the group a flat tire on their van so they wouldn't be coming. He kept talking about how it was all Satan's fault. He looked right at me when he was saying this. I can't remember if I was stoned or not but I do remember asking him if there was a Satan didn't he have more important things to do then to give a youth group a flat tire? He lost it and started screaming at me.

That night I told my parents I wasn't going back to church anymore. I was done.

Later I heard that Pastor Charlie went to another church as their youth pastor. I don't know what happened to him after that. Maybe he became a head pastor? I hope so. I always liked him and I hated lying to him. But we both knew that I had to.

EASTERN SHORE
By Mark A. Nobles

The desk was littered with a myriad of no longer sticky, sticky notes, scribbled up scraps of paper and several pocket sized composition notebooks in varying conditions of tatter. A pearl white coffee mug splotched with dribs of coffee sat on a cork coaster, which sat on a scrawled over desk calendar still showing October of last year.

I worked away on the upcoming festival with an open excel grid of the schedule, two press releases, and an open email to volunteers all fighting for room on the computer screen. My hands clickity-clacked across the keyboard. The cell phone rang.

It was early on a Sunday morning and my phone never rang on the weekend unless one of the girls was in need. I knew that was not the case as the oldest was at work and the youngest was in her room, fifteen feet away. She kept a teenager sleep schedule. I kept a feed and clothe a teenager work schedule.

The display read Unknown Caller and the area code was unfamiliar. I never answer unknown calls.

"Hello," I said.

"Hello, it's Jo Ann." Jo Ann is my dad's second wife of some forty plus years. They married shortly (my mom said too shortly) after my parent's divorce when I was thirteen. Junior high, seventh grade, 1973, platform shoes, the Cisco Kid was a friend of mine and Nixon had one foot out the door.

"They took your father to the hospital last night," Jo Ann continued in her deep south, West Virginia accent. As a Texan, that drawl was as unfamiliar and unsettling to me as the rapid cadence of a New Jersey car salesman. I never put my finger on why.

"They said he prob'ly wouldn't be coming home. I can't believe I just said that out loud." The former, Jo Ann said to me, the latter she said more to herself.

"Well, shit." I thought.

"Oh, dear." I said.

"You really must come up as soon as you can."

Besides being cold to me the few times we had ever shared air, the thing I liked least about Jo Ann, when I was a teenager, was how she ordered me, and everyone really, as if she were Joseph Smith and each word out of her mouth rose directly from Urim and Thummim and was to be followed or carried out unconditionally.

I usually took her words with the same skepticism as I took Smith and his translation.

"Let me see what I can do," I stumbled. "The festival is just over a month away. I'm swamped." This was clearly a totally unacceptable reply when you are asked to go to your dad's deathbed. I knew this.

"You simply must."

I was unprepared for this conversation and had one goal only. Hang up and end it. Deal with the consequences later.

"Let me see what I can do, Jo Ann. I will call you back shortly." There was blessed little more to the conversation and I was soon sitting back at my desk.

Thought less.

After a beat or two the girlfriend walked in from the kitchen. The house we live in is small; two bedrooms, one bath, a kitchen and a somewhat large living area. My desk is in one corner of the living area just sitting out in the open. She did not have to eavesdrop to hear every word of the phone call. Acoustically speaking, there was simply no way to avoid overhearing.

"When do you want to go?"

"I don't know that I am going."

"You have to go."

"Hell I do."

She sighed heavily; this was usually a reliable sign I was about to lose an argument.

"You aren't going for you. You're going for him," she said. "You have the opportunity to send the man off in peace."

I'm pretty sure I slumped in my chair. I'm very sure I'm o'fer in arguments with this woman. It is hard to work up a mad about it however, as I lose because I am seemingly always in the wrong. The girlfriend picks her battles carefully.

She walked over, kissed the back of my neck tenderly, squeezed my shoulder, and walked to the bathroom. I was left to sit and stew.

My dad had called a few months back with the news that he had been diagnosed with a terminal cancer. I don't remember what type, kind, or stage of cancer. It did not matter. Terminal was the key word. He had been given six to eight months. I had planned to go visit in April, after the festival was over and I had more slack in my schedule. It was an obligation trip. My dad and I had never been close. We were, as they say, estranged.

> es·tranged
> i'strānjd/
> *adjective* (of a person) no longer close or affectionate to someone; alienated.
> "Harriet felt more **estranged** from her daughter than ever."

I suppose, by that definition, my dad and I were not estranged, as I don't ever recall a time when we were close or affectionate.

I clicked around on a few travel sites looking for a flight, rental car, and a hotel near the hospital. It didn't take long to realize all the sites seemed to offer the same deals. I clicked around, looking at all the offers in detail, just the same. Stalling really, not wanting to put things in the online shopping cart and check out. I was in no rush to make this trip concrete.

I stalled, searching for an excuse not to go. I couldn't argue paucity, the girlfriend would loan me the money. I couldn't argue I was too busy, too much of a cat's in the cradle thing. There seemed no way around it. I was going to the Eastern Shore of Virginia. I found a cheap hotel within walking distance of the hospital, reserved a compact car and booked a late flight into Baltimore for Monday. At least I could arrive in the middle of the night to stave off the onslaught of seeing my dad on his deathbed and dealing with people I didn't know and had not cared to get to know for forty years.

The girlfriend called from the kitchen, "There's a big snow storm blanketing the east coast tomorrow night," she said. "You should fly in tomorrow morning or afternoon. Give yourself plenty of time to drive down from Baltimore before the roads get bad."

"Well, shit," I thought. It probably would have been a good idea to check the weather on the east coast before booking a trip from Texas in February.

The weather report was ominous. I realize Texas will shut down schools, close government offices, except for essential personnel, and barricade roads just because some Bubba spills a ten pound bag of Reddy Ice in the parking lot of a 7/11.

Repeating here, the weather report was ominous. East coast meteorologist were using the word 'blizzard' and measuring predicted snowfall in feet not inches. Still, I refused to change my itinerary. The snow was predicted to start between 9pm and midnight, Monday. My flight was predicted to touch down in Baltimore at 9:50pm.

I love the girlfriend because she recognizes male stupidity and stubbornness when she sees it, doesn't fight it, and loves me anyway.

My flight touched down at the Baltimore/Washington Thurgood Marshall International Airport a few minutes after 10pm. I was feeling pretty smug as the tarmac was dry. Not a blizzard in sight out the starboard portal on the window of the plane.

In the fourth grade when the family was stationed in Vallejo, California, my dad made me memorize certain nautical terms and naval signal flags. I came home from school one day to find a large poster of signal flags pinned to my wall. In my house mom was in the 'galley' making dinner, one went to the 'head' to defecate and Christmas vacation from school was 'leave.' Simultaneously, my mom was dressing me in paisley shirts, bellbottom jeans and I had a collection of neck scarves that would have rivaled what you would find in a gypsy vardo. This was 1968 and 69. We lived a few scant miles north of the epicenter of all things hippy. In military housing.

I was a conflicted child.

By the time I reached the rental car kiosk, snowflakes as big as the half dollar flapjacks at Ol' South Pancake House were wafting to the ground. When I approached the rental kiosk there was one clerk waiting on one customer. The terminal was empty. It had been a long flight so I stepped out the door into the cold and smoked a quick cigarette. When I reentered there was a line eight or nine people deep. Smoking is bad for your health. Addiction is an awful thing. Both complicate and harm your life in ways unimaginable to the unaddicted.

It was 11:30 by the time I was waited on. No one had gotten in line behind me. The clerk looked at my paperwork and glanced outside at the accumulating snowfall.

"Will you be driving the car much while you're in Baltimore?

"I'm not going to be in Baltimore," I replied. "I'm driving to the south end of the Eastern Shore." It was really none of his business how much driving I was going to be doing or where I was headed but I just really wanted to say 'south end of the Eastern Shore.'

"Oh," he said. In Texas he would have looked at me sideways and uttered a 'bless your heart.'

He stared at me and I stared back.

"That's no regular snowfall," he said, looking out the window at the now solid wall of snow dropping to the ground. "That is a blizzard." I felt like he really wanted to pat me on the head like I was a toddler.

"I am aware."

"Where did you fly in from?"

"Texas." I said.

"Oh." There was that tone again. "I can upgrade you to a Jeep Liberty for just an extra $5 a day."

I didn't really want to spend the extra money on the upgrade. We both turned and looked out the window. Visibility couldn't have been more than fifteen feet.

Less than ten minutes later I was on the shuttle to the garage, the keys to the Liberty in my jean's right front pocket.

The first four hours of the drive were fine. The Liberty handled well and while I was driving fifteen to twenty miles an hour under the speed limit, it was more of a visibility issue than road handling problem. I picked up an all sports talk station broadcasting from Baltimore but it turned to static about three hours in. After that I briefly picked up an NPR music station but that lasted only slightly longer than momentary. At one point I left the radio on scan for twenty, maybe thirty minutes. The cadence between mid-song, static, mid-song, static and mid-commentary, static was oddly appealing and served the purpose of keeping me alert. The road condition became more treacherous and I eased down to thirty, thirty-five miles per hour. I began to feel like I was in a snow globe being shaken by a three year old at the peak of a sugar high.

The final thirty miles took over an hour and a half. I crawled along at maybe ten miles an hour. Barely idle speed. When the sun came up it was almost a total white out. Oddly enough the landscape reminded me somewhat of West Texas; all one color, white instead of brown, capped by a crystal blue sky.

I noted my motel as I crawled past on the highway and headed straight to the hospital. I killed the engine of the Liberty a few minutes past 7am. I opened the door, stepped stiffly out and found myself standing on over four inches of packed snow and ice.

I had flown half way across the country and driven over seven hours in a blizzard to perform a task I felt, at best, less than half hearted to carry out. I walked through the revolving doors of the North Shore Memorial Hospital in Nassaawadox, Virginia feeling beat all to hell. My right ankle ached from working the gas pedal and my fingers cramped from death gripping the wheel.

I went in search of a big ass cup of coffee and my dying dad. In that order.

Day one was pretty much a waste. I was punch drunk exhausted and dad was wandering between realities in a morphine haze. Jo Ann and her youngest son were surprisingly respectful and deferential. I was given the seat next to dad's bedside. I thought that should have been Jo Ann's place but she insisted. She usually sat in whatever chair was farthest from the bed. I don't think she chose to sit so far away out of coldness but rather it was her way of coping. She didn't want to face the reality of her husband's death. She coped with it emotionally by removing herself physically. It was her way. Nothing wrong with that. People cope the best they can.

I was included in medical consultations with the doctor and nurses. I was deferred to on decisions. This was uncomfortable as I really had no idea what was medically happening to my dad. We were not close. He had called a few times and told me in vague terms what was happening. I understood it was terminal. As to specifics, I had no clue.

In laymen's terms, what I understood was dad was eaten up internally with tumors. His organs were fighting a losing battle for space and resources with these rampant growths. Nothing could be done except make him as comfortable as possible. The initial diagnosis had given him eight to ten months, but inertia was on cancer's side.

I had watched and guided my mother to her death less than a year prior. In her case I was present every step of the way. This was, in a way, familiar territory. Dealing with doctors and nurses who talked around the subject of death was how the game was played. Medical personnel hardly ever mention the inevitability death. They often simply will not say that your loved one is near the end. It is, for them, simply another phase of treatment. Jo Ann was, I think, happy to relinquish the task of dealing with these final stages to me. I had no real idea why. Maybe it was her southern code that dense, serious matters should be handled by the menfolk because womenfolk were just too delicate. Even still, her youngest son was present and he was raised from five by my dad, so really he should have stepped up. Maybe Jo Ann thought her youngest couldn't handle the weight of the situation. As my mamaw used to say, 'he ain't got much north of his ears.'

In any case, I was thrust front and center in this death spiral.

With my mother I felt it was my job, my place, to be the vanguard. Here I felt like an interloper. Like I was walking down a hospital corridor and a random family pulled me in and told me to care for their father and husband as he lay dying.

To complicate matters, dad was in a fairly incoherent state for most of the day. Hard to tell if his dementia was brought on by the heavy pain medication or was simply his present mental state. People from his church visited at regular intervals.

There were rarely less than seven or eight people in the room counting myself, Jo Ann, her youngest son and his wife. The people came and stood by dad's bedside. He mainly slept. They held his hand, looked concerned and always, always wanted to pray. Hand holding prayers. Faces lifted prayers. Heads bowed prayers. All the prayers were for a speedy and full recovery. Miracle prayers. I thought what dad truly needed from God was to be taken swiftly, mercifully and painlessly. A practical prayer.

What I mostly prayed for was not to fall asleep as by this time I was pushing thirty-six hours of tense consciousness with only hospital food and vending machine snacks to burn for energy.

What the hell. I had flown half way across the country and driven through a blizzard to do something, I guess. The sound of the girlfriend's voice kept echoing through my head, "You have the opportunity to send the man off in peace." I hung in until I could hang in no more.

I returned to the motel about nine in the evening. I was the last to leave. I considered having the heart to heart talk with dad but half the time he could only muster a mumble and the other half he was in another place, in another decade, talking to colleagues from days well gone. I called the girlfriend to touch base and passed out.

The next day was clear, sunny and well digger cold. The roads were still covered with ice but the Liberty dug in and traversed the distance to the hospital cleanly. The parade of church people continued and I was constantly praised and lauded for traveling in and braving the blizzard to see my dad. I felt like a fraud and wondered what the hell I was doing there. The roads were too bad to venture farther than my motel and there were no diners, drive-ins or dives nearby. More hospital and vending machine food for breakfast, lunch and dinner. The good news was dad was clear and lucid all day. He still slept a lot but when conscious he was present in the moment. We talked the way we always talked; about everything and nothing.

I went home around ten in the evening. Again, I was the last to leave. I reached down deep to start the heart to heart while he was cognizant and present in conversation. I simply could not do it. Feeling like a chicken shit I simply left, went to the motel, called the girlfriend and both girls to touch base and slept fitfully.

Day three, my last full day, broke clear and warm. The temperature climbed above freezing by late morning. I broke away early afternoon, determined to explore the town and find a decent place to eat. I found a little Italian place and had a good calzone. Across the street was a bakery and I loaded up with still warm muffins and a half dozen raisin oatmeal cookies to take back to my room. This was the last day to have the heart to heart. To clear the air with my dad. To send him off in peace. It was looking more and more like I just did not have this in me. I had a late morning flight from Baltimore the next day and would have to leave Nassaawadox before 6 am. I was determined to at least attempt the task. I returned to the hospital.

More chitchat with church people. More consultations with doctors. More heaping's of undeserved praise. Jo Ann and her son left around 6:30. We hugged, said we would do better about keeping in touch.

This was it. I was going to make amends with dad.

We spent the next hour talking about road conditions and how long it would take me to drive back to Baltimore.

I never felt a mental connection with my dad. When I was a kid it seemed my mom and mamaw could always tell what I was thinking. Mostly they seemed to always know when I had misbehaved, sometimes they knew what I was thinking before

I even had a chance to misbehave. But this time dad seemed to sense the moment.

I was sitting on the edge of my seat. Fumbling with my worry ring. Trying to find the words.

"I'm sorry I wasn't a better father."

I looked up, half stunned. "You weren't a bad father," I said. And it was true. He hadn't been a bad dad in the traditional sense. He was never abusive, mentally or physically. He was an absent father. That was his sin.

"I never hated you, dad. Now, in my teenage years I was mad at you quite a bit, but I never hated you."

The man was in constant pain. How much, I don't know but it was clear from the first day that the pain was ever present. When he smiled or laughed it was visible just behind his eyes. The eyes are different on people laughing or smiling through pain. Dad looked me straight in the eyes and smiled. The smile was total and complete. The pain was gone. I didn't know my dad, but I knew those eyes. They were my eyes.

He laid his head back on his pillow and that was it. Mission accomplished. I had said what he wanted to hear. The pressure in my chest began to drain like dirty dishwater down the sink.

I sat next to the bed for ten more minutes. We chatted more about my return trip the next morning. When I left I kissed him on the forehead, told him I loved him and said I would stop by briefly in the morning on my way back to Baltimore.

One more genuine, pain free smile.

I got back to the motel and sat on the bed eating a cookie. I fell asleep. The last time I glanced at the bedside clock radio it was 11:46 pm.

My cell phone rang at 12:36 am. I answered. It was a doctor at the hospital. He asked me to identify myself. I did. He paused briefly and told me dad had died about twenty minutes ago. I asked if he had called Jo Ann. He said he was about to but my name and number were first on the call list.

I asked if there was anything I needed to do. He said no. We hung up. I lay back down on the bed and was asleep in moments.

I awoke the next morning without the alarm. Gathered my belongings and loaded the Liberty. I was on the road fifteen minutes ahead of schedule.

The roads were mostly free of ice by now. I made solid, steady time. The sun rose and it was a bright, clear day. It was good to see the countryside where my dad had wound up living the majority of his life. I collect personal and place names like some men collect baseball cards. I drove through and by towns named Accomac, Little Hell, Modest Town, Metompkin, Temperanceville and Assawoman.

The Chesapeake Bay Bridge is a massive structure connecting Maryland's rural Eastern Shore to the urban Western Shore. The shore to shore span is 4.33 miles. The bridge has a reputation as being one of the scariest bridges in the world. Fearful drivers can actually pull over and a Maryland Department of Transportation employee will drive your vehicle over the span. I imagined what that job would be like, driving other people's vehicles back and forth across the bridge with them, I supposed, crouched down in the back seat, hands covering tightly clenched eyes.

As I drove across this massive bridge, I looked down 186 feet to the bay below. There were hundreds, maybe thousands, of huge broken blocks of ice jostling against each other, tossed about by the whitecaps of the icy bay water. I wondered just how large they were. From this vantage, perspective was impossible.

OUT PATIENT
By Kelley Baker

'm sitting on a London double-decker bus mesmerized by the different colors. Bright. Psychedelic. Everything is moving. People dressed in outrageous outfits. Long flowing dresses, white tuxedos, animal costumes, face paint, long hair, and beards. It's a party.

The Beatles *Hello, Goodbye* flows through speakers.

A young Ringo and I are laughing as George and John sit opposite us having a discussion about Indian spices and their effect on the body. Behind them Paul is strumming a guitar looking annoyed. Paul always looks annoyed.

This is no ordinary bus. It's the Magical Mystery Tour Bus and everyone is here. I feel great, like I'm buoyant.

The bus is packed with people, some I know some I don't. But I know the Beatles. We're old friends. It's nice to be included on this trip.

David Gilmour is taking to Mickey Rooney while Shirley Temple listens intently. Humphrey Bogart looks out the window smoking a cigarette, as Alec Guinness flirts with Natalie Wood.

Richard Nixon sobs in the corner where Albert Einstein is having a conversation with Buster Emerson from my third grade class.

People are laughing and singing, there are flowers everywhere as the sun shines brightly through the windows. We're off on a magical journey and everyone is happy to be part of it.

I soak it all in as Ringo tells another joke.

Suddenly the bus swerves, people are screaming. I'm underwater everything is harsh black and white. I can't breathe. I'm drowning. I'm fighting my way to the surface. Where's the bus? Where are the people? Where are all the colors?

"Help me! I'm underwater. I'm struggling. I'm moving but not getting anywhere. I can't breathe. I can't BREATHE. I CAN'T BREATHE!"

I wake up. I'm still groggy as I look around the room. Noisy medical equipment is everywhere. Everything's still in black and white but I'm alive!

Where am I? How did I get here? Oh God what's going on?

Ten days earlier I checked in to the hospital for a simple angioplasty. I haven't been feeling well. I've been on the road for years and it's taking its toll. I was back east when Super Storm Sandy hit. I saw the temperature drop forty-fifty degrees in less than an hour. It poured, I got soaked, and I got sick.

I'm a walker. It's how I handle stress. A morning or evening walk makes the world a better place. I'm having trouble walking. I tire easily.

One day at the Oregon coast I feel dizzy. I have to sit down. The ocean is my happy place I shouldn't feel bad here. I make up all the usual excuses, I'm tired, didn't sleep well, haven't eaten. But something is very wrong.

I schedule a visit to the doctor who sends me to a cardiologist. One failed stress test and I'm admitted to the hospital for an angiogram.

They make it sound so easy, so run of the mill. Two days before, I have a beer with my daughter who's just turned twenty-one. She asks if I want her to stay in town for the surgery? I brush it off.

"It's simple outpatient stuff. I'll be home by evening."

That's not how it turns out.

I will myself awake after the initial surgery and see my cardiologist standing next to the bed talking to a fellow I don't know.

"Mr. Baker?"

"Uh hunh…"

"The surgery went well. We found two blockages that are too close to your heart so we aren't able to put stents in. You're going to need a double by-pass. And we believe your aortic valve is leaking. This is your new surgeon. He'd like to go in tomorrow morning and fix everything."

"What? … New surgeon… Tomorrow? …"

"I'm Doctor Bradford. Looking at the angiogram I see two blockages and I can't say for certain that you're aortic valve is leaking but as long as we're in there we should look at it and if it is, replace it."

"Replace it? When are you talking about doing this?"

"First thing in the morning. I'd like to go in around 6:30."

"6:30? Don't I get time to think about this?"

"You could take 24 hours. But I think we need to do this right away."

My mind's going eleven different directions at once. What the hell? Am I that bad? Why can't I think about this? This is a huge decision? What if I die on the table? What if I die while I'm thinking about this? *IS THIS REALLY HAPPENING?*

They're waiting on my answer.

I have no insurance. I can't afford it. I've worked hard to take care of myself…

Well that's not really true. I've lived a full and fairly crazy life at times. Yes I probably drink too much, enjoy food that isn't good for me, and I get by on way too little sleep.

I work hard I play hard. I've put my body through the ringer and I've always expected it to perform. And it always has.

I guess there's a cost to all this.

I've been accused of being a workaholic, but I think I've been programmed to believe if I'm not working long hours then something's wrong. The rare times I've taken vacations I find myself checking for messages multiple times a day because I'm afraid I'm going to miss out on work.

I'm fifty-six years old and I have a few other long-term issues that I strive to control.

Holy shit! How am I going to pay for this?

When I found out I needed an angioplasty I got all of my financial shit together including two years of tax returns and went to the business office at the hospital.

"Can I help you?" said Jose.

"I'm going to be having surgery here in a couple days and I want to give you my financial records so hopefully we can work out a payment plan as I don't have any insurance."

I hand over all of the paperwork to Jose, who goes over it quickly then types something into his computer.

"I can't find when you had your surgery? What was the date?"

"Oh the surgery's in two days. The thirty-first."

"You haven't had surgery yet?"

"No."

"And you brought all of this in a head of time?"

"I try to be organized."

He looks at his computer then back at me.

"I've never had anyone bring in their financial stuff ahead of time."

I look at him foolishly, or sheepishly, likely both.

"Listen, if it's all right with you I'll hang on to all of this. I'll put it in a file. Have the surgery and then we can work things out."

"I'm worried that I won't be able to afford this."

Jose looks at me, his expression changes.

"Don't worry about that. We want you to have the surgery and we'll work it out. It's going to be okay."

I find myself tearing up.

"Thank you." I squeak.

He nods. I get up and leave before I make a real fool of myself.

Back in the recovery room they're waiting for an answer.

"Okay. If we have to we have to."

Even in my drugged state I'm afraid how much this is going to cost.

"So let's talk about your options when it comes to your aortic valve..."

Dr. Bradford explains the differences between the mechanical valve and using a "pig" valve and I opt for the "pig" valve. It seems less intrusive and also less creepy. I know you can hear the mechanical valve working and I have this picture in my mind of the Tin Man from Wizard of Oz.

My buddy Paul went through similar surgery a couple years earlier. He lives in St Louis and as soon as I find out about the angioplasty I reach out to him. He walks me through all of the steps. He's very reassuring.

I reach out to him again from my hospital bed. I text and he calls back immediately. I have no idea of the time where he is but he stays on the phone and talks me through the next steps. After an hour on the phone I'm exhausted and fall asleep.

At some ungodly hour the next morning they take me to the prep room and a hilarious woman shaves my chest and one of my legs. The leg is where they're going to take a vein to use for the bypasses. She makes me feel comfortable but once she's done I lay on my gurney alone in a hallway … waiting.

I spoke with my daughter the night before and although I try to put a brave face on everything, I'm scared. I tell her to stay at school I'll call when it's over.

As I'm wheeled in I say a short prayer. In my mind there are no atheists in foxholes, airline turbulence, and operating rooms.

"Everything's going to be okay." The anesthesiologist says as he plunges a needle in to my IV. "This is going to relax you before I knock you out."

"Do I need to count backwards or something?"

Even through his mask I can see his facial expression.

"You watch too much TV. Just relax and it'll be over before you know it."

And it is.

I wake up in the CICU (Cardiac Intensive Care Unit) to an unfamiliar face looking down at me.

"You awake?"

I nod.

"Good. I'm Bruno, your nurse. If you need anything let me know."

"Water?" I croak.

"Not yet. But you can suck on these swabs and that'll help."

Bruno has a shaved head and his arms are covered in tattoos. He doesn't look like any nurse I've ever seen before but there's something about him that I immediately trust.

"I'll be back in a few minutes."

After open-heart surgery you feel vulnerable. There is a long scar running down my chest and I'm told that my chest is wired together with stainless steel. I'm assured everything went well and in three days I'll be able to leave.

I'm taught how to get up and move around without pulling on my chest. It hurts but not as bad as trying to get up normally. I have to sleep flat on my back so my chest will heal correctly. If I sleep on my side my chest could heal at an angle, which could cause problems later on.

My surgeon, doctors and nurses, are great. They explain what's happening. But my buddy Paul's been through this from the patient side. When he talks it's easier for me to understand.

One of the things he tells me is to get off the painkillers as soon as possible. They inhibit healing. I'm lucky I have a high tolerance for pain thanks to my tough Scottish mother. She was complaining once about feeling "a bit under the weather". Three days later when my father finally got her to go to the ER her appendix was about to burst. It burst before they were able to get her in to surgery but she still recovered and went back to her normal life. She was in her late 70's.

Bruno makes sure I get up a few times a day and walk the hallways. I'm not fast but I do it and every time I push myself a little farther.

On the third day they move me out of CICU. I'm told I can go home in 24 hours if I continue to improve. I continue to look at this big gash in my chest with wires sticking out of it. In the afternoon two nurses come to remove the wires.

The wires were hooked up to a pacemaker during surgery. During the surgery they stopped my heart and then use the pacemaker to get it going again. Since I'm healing so well it's time to take the wires out. A very simple procedure.

As they're slowly and carefully pulling the wires from my chest something feels funny. I can't describe it but it feels wrong. I tell the nurses.

One of them pushes a button next to my bed and before I know it I'm placed on a gurney and rushed back to CICU.

It's bedlam! People are running around, the nurses I know are all patting me on the shoulder telling me everything is going to be fine.

One of the nurses talks to me.

"Your surgeon is in surgery at this moment and unavailable. His partner is on his way and should be here in 90 seconds. He'll explain to you what's going on."

Another doctor comes in and introduces himself. He's my anesthesiologist.

He starts yelling. "I need this! I want that!"

As I lay there surrounded by all of this frantic activity I think, "Wow, this guy's an asshole!"

Then it dawns on me. He's my asshole and this is really serious.

The other surgeon comes running in, talks to the nurse and the anesthesiologist then comes to me. We'd met before and I wondered how some high-end heart surgeon could wear cowboy boots and look so casual when my regular surgeon was a mature family man graying at the temples with a very calm disposition.

This guy is calm too. He's the center of the hurricane.

He quickly explains that one of the wires that was pulled out has possibly torn something inside my chest and he needs to go in and take care if it immediately. Does he have my permission to do this?

I realize at this moment that I might be dying.

"Yes!"

I'm handed a form to sign.

The two doctors and head nurse have a quick conversation as activity continues to swirl around me. Without warning the two doctors grab each end of the gurney, rush me down the hall, and in to a waiting elevator. They move quickly and deliberately. They speak calmly to me assuring me that everything is going to be fine.

I feel like a giant clock is ticking somewhere.

They rush me into an operating room where other people scurry about, preparing the room for surgery. The doctors disappear. More nurses come by and assure me it's all going to be fine. Their calmness helps but I find myself thinking, "Stop reassuring me, now you're scaring me!"

I lay there for a moment and focus inwards. It's the first time during this whole ordeal where I truly think, "This is it. You've escaped death a few times but this is it. I don't want to die. I want to see my kid. I want to hang out with her. I'm not ready."

Then calmness washes over me.

"Okay if this is it I've had a pretty good run. I've done a lot of great things and I have no real complaints. If it is meant to be then I'm okay with that."

I give up control. There is nothing I can do, it's all up to the doctors and nurses. I let go. The drugs are putting me to sleep. I hope I wake up.

The first face I see is Bruno, standing above me.

"You just can't get enough of me can you?"

Bruno fills me in. One of the wires did indeed tear something inside my heart and it was filling up with blood. They had around 30 minutes to get me open and start draining and fixing things otherwise I wasn't going to survive. It all went well and he'll let the surgeon know I'm awake.

After a thorough explanation from the surgeon, I'm told there's a one in ten thousand chance that what happened to me could happen. And it did. Why couldn't I have bought a lottery ticket instead of having my chest opened up again?

I'm weaker than I was when this whole thing started. I need to start all over. I'm not leaving CICU anytime soon.

I tell myself to start cutting back on pain meds. Yeah I'm in pain but I want to heal. I take a little less pain medication each time.

After a few days I'm having another problem. No bowel movements. I try but it's not happening. I'm eating but not feeling well. My stomach starts to harden and the doctors and nurses are concerned.

Except one physician's assistant. She asks me if I'm faking it? WTF? I have pain in my stomach and my bowels aren't cooperating. How the fuck can I be faking it?

It's decided that I need to have a colon procedure.

I'm knocked out again and that's when I find myself with The Beatles on the Magical Mystery Tour bus.

It's scary as hell and when I finally come out of it Bruno is there.

"You've had a psychotic incident."

"What?"

"It's the drugs. You've been knocked out a bunch of times in a short period of time and your brain is reacting to all of this. Hopefully you won't have to be put under again."

"Is this going to cause lasting damage?"

"Let's just get you well and out of here."

The rest of my stay goes without incident. Seven days later I'm released. I'm tired and weak but my heart's doing its job.

A month later I receive a bill for almost two hundred thousand dollars. I call the billing office and get Jose.

"Can you tell me exactly what happened? I thought you came in for an angioplasty?" Jose asks.

I relate to him what happened and everything I can remember, in as much detail as possible.

"Did you know I came to visit you a couple times while you were in CICU?"

"No."

"You were pretty out of it. I saw that you were still here so I figured I'd go find out what was going on. Do me a favor? Don't pay anything on this bill until I get back to you."

"I can pay a little every month."

"Let's just see what I can do. You keep recovering."

Two weeks later I receive a call from Jose.

"Are you sitting down?"

"Of course I'm still recovering."

"I've talked to the various people in charge and even took this to the board of the hospital. We're writing off your entire bill."

I'm speechless. I'm literally struggling to talk.

"Are you there?"

"Yes…" I'm crying.

"Are you okay?"

"I don't know what to say… Thank you! … Thank you."

"I'm glad to do this."

"Thank you… It seems like so little to say but it's all I can think of."

"You still owe some money to the two anesthesiologists, we don't control their billing. But I've talked to both of them and they've reduced their bills significantly and you can make monthly payments. Whatever you can pay."

I'm speechless and still crying. I struggle to say a few more things, mostly repeating, "thank you, thank you".

My surgeries were six years ago.

I'm still here and I'm healthy. I'm grateful to the people who saved my life and took such good care of me. I am very lucky.

Now if I could only remember that joke Ringo was telling me.

OUT OF THE BLUE
By Mark A. Nobles

Part One
The Bosque Place

When I was little, Ma-maw and Da-dad had a small weekend place on the Bosque River. We called it the farm, though I don't recall Ma-maw and Da-dad ever growing produce or raising animals there. Truth be known it was likely a glorified shack on a small, by Texas standards, parcel of land. It was heated by a potbellied stove and cooled by opening the windows and praying for a breeze.

On cold winter mornings I would awaken pressed between the mattress and a mountain of quilts, warm, if not slightly claustrophobic inducing. Ma-maw would holler to come get breakfast from the kitchen.

Leaving quilt mountain was hard. It took bravery and an iron will to slide from under the quilts and drop your bare feet to the slick, cold hardwood floor. But you did it and you mustered the courage quickly. There was no danger greater than not doing what Ma-maw said and doing it promptly. I don't remember much about the place other than the cold hardwood floors in winter and running the eternity from the bed to the warmth of the potbellied stove.

I do remember the top step to the back door, the only door I remember using. The first two steps were made from cinder blocks Da-dad had brought from a job site. The top step was a headstone Da-dad had found somewhere on the property. It creeped me out and I refused to step on it. Actually, no one stepped on it. My Uncle Danny said it was disrespectful to the dead. I didn't ask why it was placed there in the first place if it was disrespectful. In any case, it was too wide for me to simply step over like Uncle Danny and the grownups. I had to jump. Once, coming out the back door in a flurry, I leapt, landed wrong on the second step, and twisted my knee and face planted in the dirt.

Uncle Danny thought that was hilarious. Uncle Danny thought any misfortune that befell me was at least mildly amusing, if not outright hilarious. Uncle Danny was less than five years older than me. As an only child, he was the closest I had to a sibling.

The age difference between myself, Uncle Danny, and my mother was kind of odd when you think about it. Mother and Danny were brother and sister yet; mother was thirteen, almost fourteen when Danny was born. Most of her youth was spent as an only child. Same with Danny. By the time he was five, my mom was married and out of the house so he too was raised mostly as an only child. I was an only child, yet because dad was in the navy and sometimes stationed at sea, we spent several of my childhood years in Texas, living with Ma-maw, Da-dad and Uncle Danny.

Danny and I had spent the morning playing along the banks of the Bosque, no doubt chasing outlaws and Indians. The family dog, Suzy, a spry, red dachshund, accompanied us. She ran along side us, occasionally dashing into the brush chasing an unseen squirrel or critter of some sort.

When the sun climbed directly above us Uncle Danny declared time out and we scrambled up the bank. It was lunchtime. Best to head back to the house before Ma-maw had to shout out the back door. The Bosque was only a trickle but the riverbed was wide and steep. We climbed the bank, grabbing exposed tree roots and kicking toeholds in the soft clay. When Suzy saw us ascending the bank, she ran in a circle several times, barking up a storm, then lit out for a bend about a hundred yards downstream with smaller banks she could climb.

Geography is bigger when you are young. In my six year old mind the banks were twenty feet tall and were followed by a tree line forty feet thick, but the banks were likely less than five or six feet high and the tree line only a few feet thick.

We scrambled out of the tree line at a slow trot, Danny at the vanguard by six to eight feet. There was a massive field of Johnson grass between the tree line and house. Again, it seemed a far piece to the house in my six-year-old mind.

We had beaten down a slightly winding path in the waist high Johnson grass between the river and the house. Danny slowed to a brisk walk as we waded through. In the distance we saw Ma-maw poke her head out of the back door to call for us. Danny spotted her and waved. She retreated back in the house, the screen door making a cracking sound as it shut.

Slamming the screen door like that would have gotten me a good talking to or worse but for some reason, grownups were allowed. This seemed a mighty injustice to me.

In the distance we could hear Suzy barking her approach. I could not see her as I was barely twice taller than the grass but I could judge her distance away by the sound of her bark. We were approaching a slight bend in the beaten path when Suzy's bark rose in pitch and urgency. Danny, half way round the bend, froze. He raised his arms horizontal, palms back, signaling me to stop. But I had to see what the commotion was about and walked a few more steps.

Suzy was circling a coiled, ready to strike rattler. She ran frantically around it, breaking off every three or four rotations to run towards Danny and snap. Her running at us, teeth bared, and snapping scared me at first. She had never even hinted at biting us, but I realized the snapping was not meant to be an attack but a high warning to halt and stay away.

The rattler looked fierce. I had never seen one before. It was coiled high and made lightning strikes at Suzy when she circled. Danny cried for Da-dad and he soon came running from around the front of the house, pistol drawn. He almost always carried a pistol at the river.

When Danny saw Da-dad running he began to shout 'snake!'

When Da-dad arrived he commanded us to move back, which we immediately did, retreating back around the bend.

A single crack of the pistol sounded. Not as loud as I had expected. Da-dad took a step forward, momentarily disappeared below the Johnson grass and when he rose up he was holding the rattler by the tail end.

It looked enormous. Ten feet long. But that was impossible as Da-dad was only 5'9" and I could see the snake swinging.

Suzy got a large hunk of steak that night as a reward and the rattler decomposed on the fence line by the gate to the farm for a year.

Part Two
Lazy Afternoons

Ma-Maw and Da-dad sold their mobile home when I was in the second grade and bought a house and property in Alvarado. Over the next ten years that place became my personal Six Flags. Bound to the north by US Highway 67, a creek with a rickety handmade bridge to the east, a thicket of old oak trees to the south, and a gravel road to the west. There was a culvert, low but wide, running under 67 and a slew of Mustang grapevines that, while you couldn't Tarzan swing on them, amassed on the ground making a suitable jail cell for the cowboy outlaws that roamed my imagination. The creek walls were soft and sandy and could be easily dug out to create cave and tunnel forts for little green army men. For most of the year the forts were bombed with rocks from the creek bed chucked from the opposite bank, but for a few glorious days after the Fourth of July, they could be blown to smithereens with leftover firecrackers and bottle rockets.

Mom and I were home for the summer and half the school year as dad was stationed aboard a munitions ship off the coast of Vietnam. The Alvarado house had a long planked wooden fence that stretched from the 67 side all down the gravel road. Every three or four years Danny and I were tasked with whitewashing it. When you were holding a brush and a bucket full of paint, that fence was as tall and long as the Great Wall of China. Every morning after breakfast Danny and I were sent to the field with painting implements to spend all morning coating the fence. Suzy ran excitedly in circles leading the way. While Danny painted the inside of the fence, I painted the outside and Suzy would disappear chasing unseen and uncaught prey. Danny slapped the paint on much faster than I was able.

Ma-maw called us in for lunch at high noon everyday. Peanut butter and strawberry jam for me and peanut butter and honey for Danny. We each received a handful and a half of potato chips. Danny washed his lunch down with milk. I preferred iced tea, sometimes Kool-Aid.

After lunch the afternoons were ours. Danny usually headed off to visit a friend down the road and I skipped over to the couch to nap and watch *Dialing for Dollars*. Suzy would jump on the couch and we would drift in and out while Ma-maw did what Ma-maws do. I loved to watch the Channel 8 weatherman pretending to be a game show host and crank the big wooden drum full of postcards from viewers.

Sometimes, the movies held my eyes open, most times, they did not.

Suzy would nestle her nose under my chin and stretch her short, stubby legs across my chest. She sometimes snored worse than Da-dad. We drew breath in unison. After the nap Suzy and I would rise and head to the creek to romp and maraud until the day stretched into twilight.

I loved that dog and I loved that place.

Part Three
Trapeze

The main hall splitting the house in Alvarado had two doors on the right, the first a bathroom and the second Ma-maw and Da-dad's bedroom and two doors on the left, the first a guest bedroom and the second Uncle Danny's room. When I stayed there I lived in the guest bedroom. Our two bedrooms shared a closet with thin sliding wooden doors. I always found that to be an odd feature.

I'm not sure what Uncle Danny had done that afternoon but it had to have been a felony offense. It was a Sunday and I had been sent to my room while Uncle Danny and Ma-maw and Da-dad talked in the living room. The house had a big, open room that contained the kitchen, dining table, TV, couch and Da-dad's recliner. Most of the living was done in this area. The formal living room went mostly unused except for entertaining guests and when we were being given a severe talking to.

I didn't think it was fair that because Uncle Danny was in trouble that I had been called in with a good forty-five minutes to an hour of outside time left in the day and had been sent to my room. I was frustrated but did not put up a fuss.

After a few minutes of muffled conversation, all Ma-maw and Da-dad, I heard footsteps coming down the hall. They passed my door and went into Uncle Danny's room. It was impossible to tell at first who was walking as the green sculpted carpet disguised the heaviness of the footsteps. When they entered Uncle Danny's room, however, I knew it had to be Da-dad and Uncle Danny.

This was a belt transgression.

In a slip of a moment I heard the belt pulled from Da-dad's pant loops and a barely audible slap soon followed. Uncle Danny made no noise as a second slap quickly followed.

Suddenly the rapid gallop of Suzy's four paws sounded down the hallway. I froze. I had not heard Da-dad close the door and I knew what was about to happen.

Uncle Danny and I liked to play wrestle in the formal living room because it was open and carpeted. Suzy hated this game. She was protective of us both and it drove her nuts when we were play fighting. She would lunge and snap at me, then Uncle Danny, not knowing whom to protect. The neighborhood kids learned quickly not to lay a hand on us, even in jest, when Suzy was around, as she would snap at their calf… or worse.

I heard Suzy fly by my door. I held my breath.

Da-dad let out a high-pitched scream of terror like I had never heard. A barely coherent stream of cuss words soon followed the scream. Uncle Danny laughed, but only briefly.

"No, Suzy, down, let go!" Uncle Danny shouted.

I knew I would get in trouble for leaving my room but I had to see what was happening. I crept into the hallway and peeked in to Uncle Danny's room.

Uncle Danny was standing; hand over mouth trying to stifle laughter. His eyes were as big as saucers. Da-dad was standing, bow legged, turning in clockwise circles, swatting at Suzy, who had a death grip on the crotch of Da-dad's Dickeys Khaki pants. She was swaying to and fro like a flag in the breeze.

Ma-maw came running down the hall, brushing past me and into the bedroom. She knelt down, grabbed Suzy with one arm and with the other hand squeezed on either side of Suzy's jaw, making her loosen her grip.

"Hold still, Marvin!" She shouted.

Da-dad never ceased or repeated his stream of cursing. He also continued to twist, tangling himself with Suzy and Ma-maw. When Suzy was forced to let go, Ma-maw and the dog fell backward to the floor. It was the closest thing to a Three Stooges short I had ever seen in real life.

Suzy quickly squirmed free and ran out of the room. Ma-maw lay on the carpet laughing hysterically. Since Ma-maw was laughing, Uncle Danny felt free to let loose a giggle. I stood there, staring, with what Da-dad would later describe as a 'shit-eating grin.' Da-dad was busy giving himself and his khakis a self-examination and inventory.

Finally, through gasps of laughter, Ma-maw declared, "You know to close the door before you whip him."

"I thought you put her outside!"

Ma-maw mouthed the word 'no' and continued her belly laugh.

Part Four
Caution

As Suzy grew elderly she developed cataracts on both eyes. She got around fairly well but she moved slower and more cautious. Still, when she got excited, she had problems.

Suzy got excited about going outside and would run in circles and bolt to the door. The door to the back patio and back yard was a heavy sliding glass door that Ma-maw kept spotless. Whoa be unto anyone that did not use the handle to open the door. When I was little the door was too heavy for me to leverage open using just the metal handle. I would grab the handle with my left hand and place my right on the glass and still had to lean into it to get momentum going in my favor. Leaving prints on the glass was a worse offence than slamming the screen door at the river.

In any case, when Suzy went mostly blind she would misjudge where the sliding door was located and often slammed her little snout square into the glass, eliciting a doggie yelp. After a few collisions Ma-maw placed a 3x5 index card at Suzy's eye level that read: Caution Suzy! Solid glass door!

It was a Sunday night; Ma-maw was in the kitchen, doing what Ma-maw's do. Da-dad was in full recline position in his chair and I lay on the rug in front of the couch, playing with a couple of Hot Wheels. "Ponderosa" flickered on the television. Danny was still outside in the driveway with his 1971 red MGB on blocks, working on the engine.

Suddenly, cutting through the dialog of Hoss and Little Joe, a loud crash sounded from outside. Ma-maw let out a yelp and Da-dad shot the recliner upright and lit out like Evil Knievel off the ramp at Caesar's Palace. Da-dad was running full tilt when he smashed into the sliding glass door headfirst. He plowed straight through, stumbled, lost speed for a second, and continued out the patio and into the back yard.

Danny was fine. I do not recollect ever finding out what made the crashing noise. Da-dad suffered a broken nose, two black eyes and multiple cuts on his face and arms.

About two weeks later a second 3x5 notecard appeared on the newly replaced sliding glass door at human eye level. It read: Caution Marvin! Solid glass door!

Part Five
Worst Ride Ever with the Top Down

Not long after the cataracts developed Suzy grew a tumor on her front left leg. It was about the size of a marble when we noticed it and took her to the vet. He lanced it, bandaged it up and sent her home.

It grew back faster than before. After the third lancing the vet said he could feel other tumors in her belly. She grew listless. Da-dad and Uncle Danny had made the trip to the pound in Arlington and picked Suzy a solid year before I was born. They said she was almost a year old at the time. This put her age at over 16 years, at least.

She had about stopped eating. She mostly lay in her bed softly whimpering. Da-dad said she was suffering. Uncle Danny wrapped her in a blanket and carried her to his red MGB. I followed and got in the passenger seat. I hadn't said I was going and I had not been involved. I just got in the car. Danny handed her down to me, walked around, got in the drivers seat, started the car and pulled out of the driveway.

We sat in the vet examining room with Suzy on the metal table, her blanket under her to keep her warm. I sat in a chair parallel to Suzy, gently petting her back. The vet administered the shot and left the room. Uncle Danny bent down in front of Suzy. His face less than two inches from her cataract clouded eyes. He calmly repeated the mantra:

"I love you, Suzy."

"I love you, Suzy."

"I love you, Suzy."

She slowly ceased drawing breath.

When he was sure Suzy was gone, Uncle Danny stood vertical and gazed at the ceiling. Hands on hips. He drew three quick breaths. I stood and wrapped Suzy in her blanket. I looked at Uncle Danny. Our eyes locked for I don't know how long.

I don't remember the ride back to the house.

Epilogue

I had graduated college exactly one week prior. It was a crisp spring day and I was blasting down the interstate towards the brand spanking new film studios in Los Colinas. I had spent most of my graduation money on a three-day screenwriting class being taught in one of the massive sound stages. I was twenty minutes down the highway when I realized I had left my binder and notes back at my girlfriend's apartment. I decided it was better to be late than show up empty handed, so I took the next exit and backtracked to the apartment.

When I walked in the girlfriend's apartment she was all a tizzy. It seems less than five minutes after I left for Los Colinas, my mom had called in a flat panic. My Ma-maw had fallen due to an aneurism and been rushed to the hospital in Denton. It did not look good.

Ma-maw had been in a car wreck three months prior to my graduation. She had been laid up with multiple fractures and had just been released home the day before.

I did an about face, forgot about the screenwriting class, jumped back in the car and rushed north on I-35.

When I ran into the waiting room, I was swamped by relatives. Everyone seemed to be talking at the same time. Information was processed in fits and bits.

Aneurism. Brain. Not breathing. Twenty minutes. Revived. Coma. Brain dead.

"Just where is she?" I don't know if I screamed, shouted or whispered the words.

My cousin Kim pointed to two large metal doors. "ICU," she said.

I headed off, hit the doors but they were unyielding. I pushed and pushed. I think I slapped them once with an open palm. My Great Aunt Nita put her hand on my shoulder and pulled me back. Great Uncle Paul hit a large red button on the wall and the doors pneumatically opened.

Next I knew I was in a small ICU room full of beeping and blinking machines. Uncle Danny and my mom sat silently on either side of the bed. We all just stood and stared. After a few beats the nurse said one of us had to leave as only two people were allowed in the room at a time. Uncle Danny stood and slowly exited.

An hour, maybe two, later I stood outside the hospital with my mom as she recounted the last night's events and doctor's report. Ma-maw had gotten up in the middle of the night, sometime between 2:30 and 3 am had taken one or two steps and simply collapsed. She was not breathing by the time she hit the floor. It took the paramedics 15 to 20 minutes to arrive and another five minutes to revive her. She had been on life support ever since. Brain scans had shown no activity.

My mom and Ma-maw had a terrible fear of being stuck in 'twilight.' They would not even use the word 'coma.' I had heard them both discuss this many, many times. My mom had made me promise to never let her get stuck in twilight.

"Just let me go," she said.

"Dan won't agree to take her off life support," mom said. "We both have to agree." She was angry and frustrated. "The doctors say she'll never wake up and if she did, she would not be the same. She is already gone." It was the first conversation we had ever had were I was the grown up and she was the child looking for advice and comfort. I felt like I was wearing someone else's ill-fitting skin. We talked for a long time.

Eventually Uncle Danny relented and Ma-maw was removed from the tubes. Mom and Uncle Danny stayed in the room to wait. I sat in the waiting room with all the relatives. Styrofoam cups of coffee and Dr. Pepper cans littered the area. Three wadded up Whataburger sacks lay on a coffee table like modern art.

Mom walked through the pneumatic doors, sobbing and we all looked up thinking the same thing.

We were wrong.

Ma-maw was still breathing. Labored breathing but breathing. Mom simply could not sit for the deathwatch any longer. She collapsed in a chair. My Great Uncle Paul looked me in the eyes.

Uncle Danny and I sat silent on either side of the bed. I held Ma-maw's left hand and Uncle Danny held her right. The beeping machines and her uneven breathing formed a sort of song. The steady beeping set the rhythm and her breathes fashioning the melody. It slowed and slowed and slowed and stopped.

I looked at Uncle Danny and he met my eyes. I don't know what he was thinking and I never asked.

I was thinking of Suzy and wrapping her in a blanket to take her home.

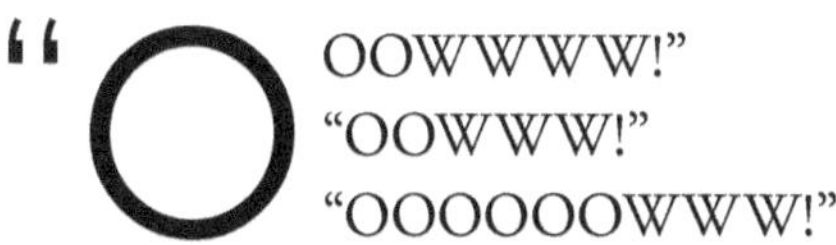

MICKEY THE DOG-FACED BOY
By Kelley Baker

"OOOWWWW!"
"OOWWW!"
"OOOOOOWWW!"

I don't like the sound of this. That's three different howls, which means at least three coyotes. I can't see them but they're close and probably hungry.

I'm as far away from home as possible on this walk. I walk faster.

My boots echo across the hard pavement. It's pushing one a.m. I'm tired and cold. On this freezing January night I'm wondering why the hell am I out this late?

I need to walk the dog.

I've been working late all week trying to get a project finished for a friend in Nashville. I'm not even close and the clock keeps ticking. I've got at least three more long nights ahead of me.

"OOOWWWWW!"
"OOWWW!"

"OOOOOOWWW!"

Judging by the howls maybe not.

Even though I'm walking faster the perspective is the same. They're following us. Naturally I'm on the only street in the neighborhood that has no streetlights.

Good ol' Portland, "the city that works" so they say. Well how about some sidewalks and a few streetlights in my neighborhood? Is that too much to ask? You pay your goddamn taxes and you hope for a couple things. I guess those cretins down at city hall are too busy with other things.

I'm too far away to try and run back to my house. And if I do will the coyotes go into chase mode? What's Mickey gonna do?

I look down at my side. The Dog Face Boy is calmly walking down the middle of the street, not a care in the world. I always knew Labs weren't the greatest when it came to protecting their owners, but he's not even paying attention!

But then I don't know him all that well. I recently adopted him from the Humane Society and I guess we never touched on how he was around coyotes?

Mickey rarely barks. It's not to say that he can't bark, or doesn't bark, he just rarely does it. Since he came to live with me he's only barked a couple times, and that was when Fiona was actively trying to get him to bark.

His bark is pretty impressive, a real window shaker. He may be ninety pounds but when he lets loose he sounds like he's at least two hundred. It's low and loud. I'm not sure where it comes from, but that bark means business.

We call him the Dog Face Boy because he has so many different expressions. My daughter and I joke that he's really a boy in a dog costume.

I'm not really scared…

"OOOWWWW!"

"OOWWW!"

"OOOOOOWWW!"

Oh yes I am. If it's three or more coyotes I have no idea what to do.

My neighborhood is one of those places that used to be more rural than suburban. On my walks I've encountered glowing eyes staring back at me from the underbrush, but those are usually low to the ground. Skunks. Raccoons. Possums.

Once a week I see homemade posters tacked on utility poles concerning missing cats that I'm pretty sure aren't ever coming home.

I'm looking around to see if I can make out anything. How close are they? How long have they been tracking us?

I've seen this one coyote before. A large male with a busted up ear. It doesn't stand straight up and there's a couple big pieces missing from it, like he tangled with something that didn't go quietly. This coyote reminds me of a bowery thug, been in a few too many fights and it shows in his face. He walks down the middle of the street during the day not caring who sees him. I haven't seen him be aggressive but I also haven't gotten close.

Without streetlights it's hard to see much and all of the porch lights are off. It's late January and Christmas lights and decorations are long gone. As much as I dislike those things I would welcome a few of them right about now.

I'm concentrating on where I walk. Did I mention this city sucks when it comes to street repair? If I trip or step in to a pothole I'm screwed.

The Dog Face Boy continues walking unfazed by any of this. What the hell kind of dog is he?

Wait a minute, maybe this is part of some larger plan? Does he have visions of running away with the coyotes instead of being a domesticated dog? I haven't had him all that long and I don't know much about his background. Maybe he was abused and that's how he ended up in the shelter? Could this be part of his revenge plan on humans?

Maybe he doesn't like the stuff I'm feeding him?

Right now all of the stupid plots of animal revenge or horror films are filling my head. If I survive this ordeal I'll buy him steak and chicken.

Why the fuck did I not take a break sooner? From here on out I'll walk the dog earlier, I promise.

"OOOWWWW!"

"OOWWW!"

"OOOOOOWWW!"

Should I knock on someone's door and ask for help? At one a.m. I'm sure they're not going to be opening the door to a guy who says he's being stalked by coyotes?

What am I going to do? I don't want to be a coyote meal?

"OOOWWWW!"

In the middle of a long coyote howl Mickey stops. He turns his head and looks back up the street in the direction the howling is coming from.

All of a sudden he lets out two of the loudest barks I have ever heard. Two Window Shakers! These barks aren't hostile, they're not aggressive, but they aren't friendly either. The hair is up on his back.

The howling stops immediately.

Mickey slowly turns his head forward and looks around.

I'm scanning the darkness as well.

Mickey sniffs the air for a few moments.

Finally he looks up at me. He wags his tale and I see in the Dog Face Boy an expression that says, "Don't worry, I got this."

He turns and with his tail wagging ever so slightly continues along on our late night walk.

I don't hear any more howling.

We have a very quiet and uneventful walk back home. The Dog Face Boy is taking his time, stopping, sniffing, and marking. He's in no hurry.

We encounter the big coyote with the mangled ear a few days later on one of our early morning walks. He freezes and looks squarely at Mickey. Mickey stares right back. He is absolutely silent but I see the hair on his back is up.

This stand off lasts maybe ten seconds, then the coyote turns and goes back the way he came. I feel Mickey relax and we continue our walk.

That's the last time I've seen or heard any of the coyotes in the neighborhood. I know they're still out there, and they know Mickey is still walking with me.

The Dog Face Boy still rarely barks. He doesn't need to.

POT ROAST FROM VANCE GODBEY'S
By Mark A. Nobles

The Hayloft on Jacksboro Highway didn't have an outside light over the door, let alone a pole light in the parking lot. The sign atop the dilapidated building was barely recognizable as a sign at all, being as it was only half a sheet of rotted plywood on which Inez's third husband, Dick, had scribbled 'Hay Loft' in black paint with a four-inch brush.

Dick had caught hell for the misspelling and Inez had kicked his ass to the curb less than two weeks later, not for that specific transgression, but it had been the next to last one she allowed. It was best for all concerned if one did as Inez instructed, exactly as Inez instructed, not part way or close.

It was a one ambulance night on Jacksboro, unusually slow for a Tuesday, and even more so in the Hayloft. Inez was behind the bar reading yesterday's editorial page of the Fort Worth Press and smoking an unfiltered Camel which was, at this point, more curved ash than tobacco and paper. Inez was 4' 11" and of unknown weight, but she had to be under 100 lbs. She wore whatever the hell she wanted, and her beehive was a full 15 percent as tall as she.

On the bar to her right a mostly eaten plate of pot roast, mashed potatoes, corn, and pea salad, sat congealing. Buddy, who spent almost as much time in the Hayloft as Inez, had brought the food to her from Vance Godbey's Barbecue, which was up Jacksboro, almost into downtown. Truth be told, Godbey's barbecue wasn't much to write home about, but his wife's pot roast was better than your mama's pot roast and I don't care who your mama is.

Willie sat at a table picking strings and bits of songs nobody knew. Buddy was molding his butt to his regular barstool and a first timer sat at a table in the furthest corner of the room. Inez was suspicious of first timers, so she kept her radar on him. She knew he sat where he did just to make her hike his Pearl across the room. That put him two strikes down and he hadn't been in the Hayloft 45 minutes.

"Don't you know any happy songs, Willie?" said Inez.

"No, ma'am," Willie sang. Even when he talked, Willie sounded like he was singing. "But I'll make one up for a Jax."

"Hell," the man in the corner interrupted, "I'll buy you a beer and a shot if you'll shut the hell up."

Everyone turned and stared at the stranger in the corner except for Willie, who put down his guitar, and sat up straight in his seat.

"I'll give Willie his beer and back but only to make you pay," said Inez. "and I'll thank you to be more cordial to my customers."

"I drove into Fort Worth from Mineola for the Fat Stock Show and heard tell this was the place to meet rasslers and ain't nobody here but a midget barkeep and two alchies," said the man.

The Hayloft was not lit up like Christmas because it had its own built in clientele, mostly wrestlers, roustabouts, and carnies, both from here permanent, and those traveling through. Inez hadn't meant for the Hayloft to be a home for wrestlers and roustabouts, it just happened. She didn't mind because they always had cash, had already got fighting out of their blood before they came in the door, and most were more polite than you'd think. They all liked Inez because she served full drinks, made fair change, and treated them like they were regular folk.

Inez drew Willie's beer and poured his shot. Willie knew better than to make her bring the drinks to him, so he stood, grabbed his guitar and walked to the bar.

"Don't pay him no heed, Willie. I like the way you play."

"I know you do, Inez." Willie threw back the shot and shook. He wasn't used to anything but rotgut whiskey and Inez had poured a shot of the good stuff, since the man in the corner was paying the tab. "He's right though."

"I'm willing to bet that asshole hasn't been right since he was shitting himself in diapers," Inez cut her eyes at the man in the corner. "You've got talent, Willie, that isn't the question," she looked back to Willie, and gazed into his sad, hazel eyes. "Maybe the nightlife just isn't for you."

"It ain't no good life, that's for sure."

"It's no way to live, Willie, out here playing songs for drinks, especially when you've got a good woman like Martha at home."

Willie stood a full head taller than Inez, but that didn't put him much more than 5' 6."

"I get restless when the evening sun goes down," he said. "There's no place for me, so I guess this is my life."

"Well, I'll repeat what you said back to you. It ain't no good life, Willie, bumming around on Jacksboro. You ought to march your ass home, get Martha, and take her to the courthouse first thing in the morning and marry her before she comes to her senses."

"Marriage hasn't done you much good, Inez."

Inez laughed, raised her hands in mock protest and said, "It's done me a world of good, that's why I do it so often." They both laughed. "And I'm looking to marry again. It's hard running a bar by yourself."

"How many husbands you already had?" Willie asked.

"Four," she replied. "If you don't count one repeat and two licenses I didn't use."

The man in the corner suddenly began to belt out the first verse of 'If You've Got the Money I've Got the Time.'

Inez cut him off, "What in the hell are you doing?"

"I need a drink and I figured the only way to get one around here is to squeal a country song like a stuck pig," bellowed the man in the corner. "I'm the paying customer and I can't get another round?" The man in the corner raised his empty mug and slammed it on the table for emphasis.

Inez pulled a Pearl from the cooler, snapped off the top and began to head around the bar. "I'll get you another beer, but I think you best settle your tab and drink it on the road."

"I'm not going anywhere until I meet a rassler," the man insisted.

"It's Tuesday," said Inez, "we don't get many of those boys in on Tuesdays." Inez slapped the bottle on the man's table. "Some are family men, home with their wives, or they're on the road traveling to next weekend's match or healing up from last weekend's injuries."

"Healing up," the man snickered. "Ain't none of them Nancy boys healing up."

Inez raised up stiff as a board, it might have been the only time in her life she stood a solid five foot tall. She was taken aback. Inez is never taken aback. "What the hell did you say?"

"You heard me," he stared Inez dead in the eyes. "None of them Nancy boys is healing up because none of them is hurt. You don't get hurt fake rassling."

Buddy, who had been doing the crossword out of the paper, put down his pen and slowly looked around. "Sheee," he exhaled. Buddy ran out of breath before getting around to enunciating the 't'. Willie grinned and pick up his guitar and softly started strumming what sounded like a cross between a hymn and a dirge.

Inez loomed over the man's table, "I don't think you know what you're talking about, so I'm willing to let it go."

"I wrestled in high school and I watch a lot of TV rassling, so I do know what I'm talking about. It is fake and I'm pretty sure at least some of them just enjoy rolling around with other men and get paid for it."

"Listen buster,"

"The name's McGill," the man said. "If you'd cared to ask."

"I don't care and I'm not interested in your name, buster," Inez continued. Willie's eyes glowed as he continued to play. Buddy slid off his stool and slowly walked around behind the bar and hunkered down.

"Sure, a man can be a face in one town and a heel in another, that's part of the show, and some are pushed more than others, but what goes on inside the ring is real."

"That ma'am, is pure manure."

"Is this manure," said Inez. She then proceeded to grab the man and execute a perfect falling arm drag, landing the man on the bare concrete floor.

"Ooof." The suddenness of the landing had expelled most of the air from the man's lungs.

Inez was just warming up.

"I learned that from Ruffy Silverstein." As the man got to his knees, she followed up with a textbook karate kick. "That ain't exactly the way Duke Keomuka showed me but I ain't got the heft he does."

The man was laid out face down and slid a good four feet across the floor. Inez calmly walked over and grabbed the man's right leg and placed his ankle between her thighs. She then laid on top of his back and locked his arms around his head. She pulled back stretching the man's back, neck, and knee in a most unnatural way. The man had no time to refill his lungs with air, so his scream was silent but written all over his face.

"This rassling move is called the stepover toehold facelock," Inez wasn't even breathing hard, but her eyes betrayed her rage. "I learned it from Lou 'Iron Man' Thesz, and I know I'm doing it mostly right because he invented it." She gave another fierce tug on his leg. The man inhaled, gasped, and screamed all at the same time, which seems like a physical impossibility, but it happened.

She let go his leg and he moaned and rolled over. He was attempting to get up, but he just wasn't able. Inez rose to her feet and took four deliberate steps away. "You're not selling the moves, buster, but that's alright." She turned on her heels, swung her arms back and strode towards the man, on the fourth step she leapt high in the air, slightly tucking her knees on the way up, causing a rotation of her tiny body. She landed solid on the man, her back to his stomach.

At that point it was over and too gruesome to describe.

"That fake move is called the bombs away," Inez said getting back to her feet. "Jack the Giant Killer learned me that one." Inez checked that her beehive was still straight on top her head as she walked back to the bar. Buddy, sensing the all clear, peeped up, and Willie changed his tune to a slow country waltz.

"Now, I ain't saying there isn't some show in the show," Inez continued. She grabbed her Camels and shook one out. Buddy slid a pack of matches down the bar. She caught it, extracted a match, struck it, and lit the cigarette. "There's jobbers who've only ever taken a squash and they've made good money and had long careers, but if you don't think the rassling is real," she paused and looked at McGill. He had not moved in a while. "Say, are you still with me?"

A low moan was all he could muster to indicate that Inez had his attention. "Okay, good. I thought we might have lost you. As I was saying, there might be a push for one man over another but if you think the rassling is fake, well, you're plain wrong. And if you want to see 'real' rassling, catch a rassler after a screwjob," Inez chuckled heartily. "That's some rassling. A real smark can tell."

McGill's voice was weak and cracked. "I don't know what you are saying, but please believe me when I tell you I know what you mean."

Inez took a long drag on the Camel. "I believe you do, Mr. McGill from Mineola."

The bar was silent for several moments. Buddy went back to his crossword and you could almost hear Inez's Camel burn to ash.

"You going to drink that, mister?" Willie asked politely, pointing to the man's beer.

The man did not speak but managed to shake his head 'no.'

Willie looked to Inez. Inez shrugged. Willie quit playing, stepped over the man to get to the table, and picked up his Pearl.

DIRTY BIRD IN A BATH
By Kelley Baker

"**B**ourbon and water please."

"That's an old man's drink." says the bartender as he winks at me.

Just what I need a chatty bartender. It's been a long tough day and I got a call earlier from my apparently soon-to-be ex-wife. I guess I'm a pretty horrible person. I just want some quiet and to be depressed in peace.

Quick as a wink my drink is sitting in front of me. I nod not wanting to engage. The bartender has other plans.

"You know what we used to call this?"

I shake my head.

A Dirty Bird in a Bath. Old Crow and water."

I say nothing.

"Never seen you here before?"

"I could say the same." I reply.

"I'm here just two nights a week. It keeps me busy. Michael Sullivan." He says with a hint of an Irish accent, as he extends his hand.

Michael's in his late sixties wearing a white shirt with a neatly pressed black vest, black slacks, bright white hair, and a twinkle in his blue eyes that's pure mischief.

Not surprising he has a firm grip.

"I'm Sean."

"Now that's a good Irish name." He says.

"I wouldn't know I'm Scottish."

"It's a fine Celtic name no matter what part of the island you're from."

Obviously he can't tell that I'd prefer to be left a lone. I could tell him to buzz off but I wasn't raised to be rude. Hopefully someone else will come in and he can go talk their ear off.

"So what are you doing in town?"

"I'm working on a film and this is where they put me up."

"You an actor?"

I shake my head. "Just one of the grunts."

"Do you like it here?"

"It's a little rich for my blood but somebody else is paying so I'm good with it."

"We get some interesting folks that's for sure."

"You been here a while?"

"About a year. I used to have my own place in the city, but I closed it. I thought I'd retire but I found I needed something to do."

Michael spreads his arms wide behind the bar.

"And this is all I know. I hate watching TV, and I missed interacting with people."

"Even the ones who stay at a fancy place like this?"

"You're here. Besides they're all interesting. I just sit back and listen, I don't have to go home with any of 'em."

Michael notices I need another drink and it's in front of me before I know it. I didn't order it, but I'm not complaining either. If I have to talk to someone tonight it may as well be a bartender.

"So where was your place?"

"North Beach. Just down from the Condor Club."

"The Condor Club? With Carol Doda?"

"Those were the days. I'd get a lot of the overflow when she was in her heyday."

"You had dancing?"

"Oh no! It was just a little Irish Pub called Sullivan's. A nice quiet place to drink. Most nights anyway."

"Were you there when the hydraulic piano came down and crushed that guy?"

"I was. That's not a good story. Carol would come in sometimes after closing and we'd have a cup of tea together. Nice lady. Loved a good cup of tea and conversation."

"That's amazing. Tea with Carol Doda…"

Michael smiles quietly lost in the memory.

"Anyone else come in that I might have heard of?"

"Hard to say. Nobody remembers those times."

"Oh man, I do. I loved that period of time. I missed it by about twenty years. North Beach was such a wild place. Did the beats come in?"

"They did. Allen was quite polite and very soft spoken. I liked him a lot. Neil could be quite the gentleman, he helped out at the bar some nights. And very handy if something broke."

"It's hard to imagine all of those people in one place. Did Kerouac ever come in?"

Michael nods.

"If he was drunk, and he usually was, he'd get belligerent. I tossed him out on more than one occasion. The other guys always apologized for him. I never liked him and I couldn't get through his books."

"Was there really that "anything goes" feeling in those days?"

"Among some. Mostly outsiders. I just ran a neighborhood bar with good music on the jukebox and good whiskey by the glass. I lived round the corner back when you could afford to. Raised my kids there."

"It's too bad you closed. A lot of history there, with the Beats and all."

"It was a good time. Mostly."

"Do you miss it?"

"I miss people, not places. The neighborhood changed. The old guy who owned the building died and his kids sold it to some investors who raised my rent ten-thousand percent. My kids were all grown so I moved in with my daughter and her husband in Oakland."

Michael smiles, then moves off to help one of the bus boys carrying a load of clean cocktail glasses from the kitchen.

An older couple comes in and takes a table by the wall. Michael takes their order and is back with their drinks in a flash.

I sit at the bar and stare at my drink. I've totally forgotten about my shitty day. I'm tired and need to go upstairs and get some sleep. I also wanna sit and talk with Michael but I have an early day tomorrow.

"Another?" Michael asks.

"No. I'm gonna settle up and call it a night."

I pull out my wallet.

"Your tab is settled."

"What?"

"I hope tomorrow goes better for you." he says with a smile. "Get some rest. And if you wanna know if a bartender knows their stuff, ask for a Dirty Bird in a Bath."

Michael walks off.

"Next time I want to hear more stories about Carol Doda." I call after him.

I lay down enough cash for a healthy tip.

I check in to the bar a few more times over the next few weeks but don't see Michael.

A year and a half later I'm mixing another film and staying at the same place. The first couple weeks we're behind schedule. I'm working late every night, no time for hotel bars.

Anna, the post-production supervisor from the studio arrives with two junior studio executives. They don't look happy and I can see she's worried. She tells me to meet them for dinner at the hotel restaurant, as there are some things to discuss.

They're all impatiently waiting with their cocktails when I finally show up out of breath. The executives are annoyed and Anna is stressed.

As I sit down the waiter asks what I want to drink.

"A Dirty Bird in a Bath." I say without hesitation.

The executives look at me wondering what I've ordered but don't ask.

"Shall I tell the bartender what's in it?" asks the waiter.

"Any good bartender should know." I reply.

The executives start in on how we're behind schedule and over budget, which was true before I started on the film. They're trying to intimidate me.

"How are you gonna deal with getting this movie back on track?" One of them demands.

"You need to get everyone to work faster and longer and we're not paying overtime. We don't want to spend any more money than we have to."

None of this is my responsibility but apparently I'm the fall guy.

"Why aren't you talking to the producer or the director?"

"Because you set the pace."

Which is not true. But they're just warming up. It's going to be a long meal.

"We have a lot invested and we want some accountability…"

From behind me I hear a familiar Irish accent.

"I knew it was you. How are you doin Sean?"

I turn and there's Michael. He's brought my drink into the restaurant personally.

"I'm just checking to see if the bartender knows what he's doing."

"He's a good man but he's never known what he's doing? He can still make a good stiff drink though."

"He always could. How's Carol?"

"She's alive in my memories."

I shake his hand and we talk for a moment about Carol Doda and the Beats as the executives glare.

After a few moments I give Michael a hug.

"I'll come by later. You still owe me some stories."

"And I have some good ones for you."

With a twinkle in his eye, Michael stares at the executives for a moment. Finally he says, "You take good care of this guy, he's my friend."

He slowly turns and walks away.

I sit back down at the table and the whole atmosphere changes.

"How do you know him?" One asks.

"He seems familiar." says the other.

There is a long pause.

"So about speeding up the mix…" I say.

Both executives look back at me like they forgot I was sitting there.

"Don't worry about it. It's all gonna work out. Let's enjoy dinner shall we?"

When the waiter comes back they order a round for all of us and the film is not brought up for the rest of the meal.

They leave the next day and Anna assures me everything is good.

I see Michael a few more times while I'm staying there. No matter how busy he is he always has time to tell a good story.

The last few times I stayed at the hotel Michael was no longer there and no one seems to know what happened to him. They all agree he knew how to brighten up the place and make you forget about your troubles without even asking. He is missed.

Michael, I have no idea where you are or even if you're still walking the earth. But I remember your voice and the twinkle in your eye. I haven't added water to my whiskey in a long time.

Tonight I'm pouring myself a Dirty Bird in a Bath and I'm toasting you, wherever you are.

"May the winds of fortune sail you,
May you sail a gentle sea.
May it always be the other guy
who says, 'this drink's on me.'"
- - Old Irish Proverb

THE MAN IN DICK VAN DYKE'S HAT
By Mark A. Nobles

The man leaned against the Knights of Pythias Building in downtown Fort Worth and seemed oblivious and invisible to the bustle about him.

Don't get me wrong, he wasn't invisible, he was there all right. It's just he and each and everyone else walking by was encased in their own personal bubble. All unaware of each other.

The man was in bad need of a shave and his clothes had seen a lot of miles. He wasn't dirty so much as unkempt. He was dressed like he had two part time jobs, one as a circus ringmaster and the other a maître d' at a restaurant where the prices are not printed on the menu. He wore a tattered, battered, and torn straw hat that once belonged to Dick Van Dyke. Everyone's seen it. It was the one Van Dyke wore in *Mary Poppins*. Not one like it, the very same hat. The man and Van Dyke had been friends at one time.

But that is a different story.

This is my Uncle Paul's story. Great Uncle Paul to be genealogically precise. He was my maternal grandmother's brother in law.

Uncle Paul was my favorite uncle. He looked out for me. He was about the only male relative I had who spent much time with me. It was Uncle Paul who taught me how to tie my shoes. He showed me how to kick a ball. Most importantly, he answered my boyhood questions.

My father was absent most of my childhood and my grandfather, I called him Da-dad, was, well, a man of few words. Da-dad spoke in concise, blunt sentences, most of which were either declarative or imperative.

Uncle Paul was career Army and did four tours in Vietnam. The first two tours he was ordered to go. The last two tours he volunteered.

On the day before Uncle Paul was to leave for his fourth tour. Aunt Nita was pissed. For weeks I had heard her and my mom talking about Uncle Paul leaving. Aunt Nita was worried and scared. She did not want him to go. She did not understand why he kept volunteering to go back.

It was 1967 and young men were avoiding the draft by heading over the border to Canada in droves and most career Army personnel were hunting cushy, safe deployments stateside. Meanwhile, Uncle Paul had already been in combat three times and returned from each tour without a scratch. Aunt Nita felt Uncle Paul was pressing his luck.

This was a time when the news, radio and TV broadcast daily death and casualty tolls. Film of the carnage was shown every afternoon and evening, promptly at 5 and 10 pm. There were signs of protest everywhere and the legitimacy and winnability of the whole war was being called into question.

I didn't understand the political or social ramifications. I was six at the time. I just knew my mom and Aunt Nita were concerned about the safety and life of my Uncle Paul.

It was a Sunday afternoon and everyone was outside eating barbeque and drinking beer. I was inside Aunt Nita and Uncle Paul's singlewide mobile home out near Pelican Bay, morosely playing with my little green army men. Uncle Paul came inside and sat down on the rug next to me.

"What you got going on there?" he asked.

"Just playin'," I replied.

"You seem off your feed. You barely ate and I've seen you put away half a side of beef as a snack."

I shrugged my shoulders. "I'm just not hungry, I guess."

"Something on your mind?" Uncle Paul looked me in the eyes and would not let go.

"I heard that one of these times you are going to the war and not coming home."

Uncle Paul sighed and looked at the ceiling. When he returned his gaze to me he reached down and grabbed one of my little green army men; the one frozen in a running crouch with his carbine clutched across his chest. "You see this fellow?" He asked me.

"Yes, sir."

I had the little green army men broken into two groups facing off against each other. Uncle Paul placed the running soldier behind the line of the group closest to me, running away from the fight. "If there is ever trouble over there, this will be me," he said.

I giggled.

"So if I were to get hurt, it'll be here." He tapped the little green army man three times on his butt. I covered my mouth and giggled again. Butt jokes are funniest when you are six.

"You understand, now?" Asked Uncle Paul. He set the green army man back on the floor but still running away.

"Yes, sir."

"Want to come out and get some potato salad? I saved you some."

"You bet." I scooped up the little green army men, placed them in my cigar box and ran outside with my Uncle Paul to fill that hollow leg my mom said I had with potato salad and brisket.

Years later Uncle Paul and Aunt Nita still lived in the mobile home park near Pelican Bay. The singlewide had been replaced with a double wide sometime in the mid 1980s. Aunt Nita had developed dementia.

One time she almost burned down the trailer by placing her purse on the stove and turning on the burner. She thought she was boiling water for tea. Another time she had gone to get cigarettes at the 7/11 on Jacksboro highway and wound up on a lonesome Farm to Market road in Parker County.

I didn't go out to see them as much as I should. Hell, truth be told, I hadn't gone out there in years, definitely not since Aunt Nita had begun to slip. My mom finally shamed me for my negligence so I made the trip out late one Saturday afternoon in the fall.

It was a sad, mustard yellow sunshine afternoon. Aunt Nita was completely separated from the here and now but was mostly listless and sat in her recliner. At least that made it easier for Uncle Paul to look after her. Uncle Paul's jet black pompadour had turned silver but was still a solid 3 to 4 inches tall. I made a pretense of communicating with Aunt Nita and then Uncle

Paul and I went outside to sit in the metal, seashell backed patio chairs. The chairs had been on that patio since the singlewide days and at one time had been a festive bright orange but most of the color had drained away.

"What have you been up to lately?" Asked Uncle Paul.

"Working, traveling quite a bit."

"Your mom says you've hooked up with some older woman. She strongly disapproves."

"I bet she voiced more than strong disapproval."

We both chuckled. My mom was married to a sailor for years and the joke was she likely taught him more than a few new cuss words. I grabbed two beers from an ice chest, handed one to Uncle Paul and then plopped myself down next to him. We popped the tops and continued talking.

"But that's good you're traveling, getting out more. You spent a long time hiding out at your mom's. It's good you are getting back out in the world."

Uncle Paul was referring to my dark years. In college, a group of friends and I had made a beer run late one night and hit and killed a man on the drive home. It had been dark, we were all drunk and I was driving too fast. He came into the headlights out of nowhere and just stepped into the road. The collision killed him instantly.

I heard the sound of his bag of bones hitting the fender, then the hood, then the windshield, then the pow, pow, pow as he rolled over the roof of the car every time I closed my eyes. Even to blink.

The police eventually ruled it a suicide. The man purposefully stepped in front of my car. They found a note in his jean's pocket.

I spent the next three years contemplating why he picked me to end his life. I dropped out of school and moved back in with my mom. Lots of therapy and a little prescribed and self-medication later I was finally getting my mind right. Driving from the south side of Fort Worth all the way out to Pelican Bay was one of the longer drives I had made behind the wheel and on my own.

The visions were slowly getting sorted and stored away.

"I'm still making bad decisions, but they're my decisions," I said.

"You're young. Bad decisions are all you know how to make at your age."

Uncle Paul sat in his chair, picking at the rust on the armrest. "Things that can't be unseen are the most difficult to describe," he said.

I looked at him blankly. I had no idea what he was talking about or what he meant.

When Uncle Paul saw my puzzled gaze, his look turned a little sheepish. "Some things can be hard to live with is what I mean. They're like women, you know? Can't live with 'em, can't live without 'em."

"Oh, believe me, I'm doing my damnedest to live without these," I said. "I'm sure in Vietnam you saw way more and way worse than I have, Uncle Paul. But you managed. I will too. Eventually." I hung my head, trying to find a way to change the subject.

I didn't want to talk about the accident, years of therapy and what I considered to be wasted time flailing aimlessly trying to get back my sanity. I didn't want to talk about Aunt Nita. It seemed I didn't want to talk about anything in the here and now.

I looked at the rusted 1969 El Camino languishing on cinder blocks in the yard. If I had known anything, anything at all about cars, I would have asked about the restoration project even though I knew he hadn't turned a wrench on it in over a decade. Work had stopped after Uncle Paul's oldest son died in a head on coming home from working the third shift at the bomber plant.

One way to tell how long someone had lived in Fort Worth was by what they called the aircraft plant that sat right next to Carswell Air Force Base. If they called it GD or General Dynamics, they were newbies. The old timers still called it the bomber plant and some even still referred to it as Convair or Plant Number Four.

"There is something you need to know," Uncle Paul said, looking down to his lap. He fidgeted in his chair a bit. "I'm glad you came out today. I've been thinking a lot about you. This is gonna sound funny, but… Well, but, I'm afraid for you." It was like it took all the strength he could muster to say that last sentence. I was touched he was worried about me but puzzled as to why he would be afraid.

It crossed my mind that maybe Aunt Nita wasn't the only one in the double wide with a touch of dementia.

"Uncle Paul, I'm fine. I just need to chase these ghosts or learn to live with them. Lock them up somewhere in my head."

I know. Lord, I know. But that's my fear. I believe you can come to terms with what you have seen. You've put in a lot of work sorting things through. I just don't ever want that work to be undone."

"I don't understand."

Uncle Paul looked around the yard as if he was afraid we were being watched. It was midday on a Tuesday during the spring. The adults in the trailer park were at work and the kids were in school. The place was a redneck ghost town.

"You likely will think I'm crazy but that don't matter. All you have to do is remember what I tell you. Just remember." He looked me dead in the eyes. He was serious as a heart attack.

"I'm listening," I said.

Uncle Paul continued to stare me down.

"And I promise I'll remember," I said.

"Alright then."

Uncle Paul took a breath and held it. It was as if he was mustering his strength again. Collecting and organizing his thoughts.

"I want to tell you a story you are going to have a hard time believing. But every word is true."

He picked on the armrest rust some more, took a quick pull on his beer and dove in. "It was 1973 and I had gone downtown to pay a ticket I had gotten on Jacksboro Highway. I was walking back to my car, the sidewalk was empty, as far as I can remember, when all of a sudden, he was standing right in front of me." Uncle Paul paused to let his memory catch up to his words.

"Who was in front of you?" I asked.

"I don't know who he was. I don't know what he was." Uncle Paul's almost golden brown eyes hazed over like the memories he was conjuring were cataracts. "He looked kind of like a Traveler, but I don't think he was. His breath smelled like moth balls, spoiled milk, and fear."

Uncle Paul wrinkled his brow as if he had to wrangle his thoughts before he could continue. He stopped picking at the rust and clenched his fist.

"We were standing there on the sidewalk. Face to face, less than 12 inches from nose to nose. His eyes were lightening blue with silver flecks." He paused again re-seeing those eyes in his mind. "Those flecks looked like West Texas stars and they floated and swirled in the blue like flecks in a softly shaken snow globe." He paused again reliving the memory.

"'Want to see something interesting?' The man said to me. 'It won't cost you a dime. Only your time.' He said, like a barker at a carnival."

Uncle Paul was lost in the memory now. I was confused as hell but didn't want to shake the spell.

"Well, I knew he was telling a lie. Like I said, he looked like a Traveler or a carnival barker and carnies and Travelers always have their hands in your pockets but I had already been to the courthouse and they had taken every dime I had, so when he turned and started to walk down the alley, I followed. I admit he had my curiosity up." Uncle Paul drained his can of beer and shot me a glance to see if I was maybe thinking he was crazy. What he saw in my eyes was love, concern, and confusion. He looked a little relieved and continued.

I got up, went over to the cooler and fetched him another beer. Just like the old days when I was a kid.

"Thank you, son." He took the can, popped the top and continued talking. "We walked about halfway down the alley and stopped in front of this little wall of cotton candy. Now, I know how this sounds but it's true. It is all true." Uncle Paul paused for effect.

He leaned towards me and pointed his beer can hand at me to emphasize his point. "It was goddamn cotton candy because he pinched off a corner and ate it. It was just floating there. Goddamn cotton candy. The pink kind."

I laughed, then he laughed. I was hanging on to every word. I had questions. Shit tons of questions, but I didn't want to stop the flow.

"I stood in front of the cotton candy, right next to this guy and all a sudden images started to appear inside the cotton candy. Murky at first. Just floating, slowly taking form. It'll sound weird, but hell, this whole thing sounds weird, but the images weren't really coming from inside the cotton candy. They were coming from inside my head. They were my images or rather, my memories. Memories I had long since buried. But I didn't see them in my head like a memory; I didn't see them until they appeared in the cotton candy. It was like they were being projected from inside my head, onto or into the cotton candy. They were images I had forgotten. Images I had locked away in order to keep my sanity. Suddenly they were released and projected and I had to re-watch them. Relive them to put it more accurately."

Tears began to journey down Uncle Paul's cheeks. We weren't laughing anymore. Uncle Paul sat in his chair and mildly shook. Sweat formed on his forehead and cheeks, mixing with the tears and rolled down to his jawline.

The story, as they say, had taken a turn.

Uncle Paul wasn't in that back alley with the strange, carnival dude any longer. He was back in Vietnam. "It isn't the gore and violence that unnerves you. Maybe for some people it is but it never was for me. It is the possibilities and all the consequences of all the possibilities. It gets in your head and eats it like termites gnawing on wood."

Uncle Paul paused to gather his thoughts. I wasn't sure he was talking to me anymore.

"In any case, something happened different with me in that alley. Wires got crossed. A monkey wrench got thrown into the works. I don't know but I do know something went wrong." Uncle Paul thought hard for a beat or two.

"Maybe gremlins." He looked at me hoping to see some sliver of understanding. Then, I think he decided he didn't care if I understood. Just saying what he had to say was enough. His eyes darted downward.

"Gremlins are real, you know." He said with authority. "Ask most anyone who's been in combat. On second thought, don't bother because they won't tell you unless they know you've been in combat."

"Are you talking gremlins like that Twilight Zone with William Shatner?"

"The Captain Kirk guy?"

"Yeah."

"Exactly, yes. That story is real. It has to be. I think maybe that narrator guy…"

"Rod Serling," I interrupted.

"Did he serve in combat?"

"I'm not sure." Uncle Paul looked disappointed. Then he continued.

"I bet he did because I think he's met the man, too, like me, because a lot of those stories he writes are real or could be real. Only difference is he's making money off it, I'm just tortured by nightmares."

"Why did you go to Vietnam so many times when you didn't have to?"

"I fucking hated it. You have to understand that first. I fucking hated the whole situation." I had never heard Uncle Paul utter the F word. This was almost as unsettling to me as the rest of his story.

"But it was something I had to do. They were sending children unprepared over to Nam to be slaughtered. Pure and simple. Running around in the forest in Georgia does not prepare you for being dropped in the jungle. They could have at least kissed them before screwing them over. I was older. I had been there before. I knew how to survive. I went back to try and bring at least a few of them back home with me. It seemed the decent thing to do. Sometimes you need to worry about more than just your own ass."

Uncle Paul grunted and grabbed his head. I didn't know if it was from pain or frustration.

"But like I was saying. Something went wrong. I think I was only supposed to remember the visions of Vietnam. But I remembered more. I remembered the man."

Uncle Paul went silent. We sat there motionless. Two men in rusted metal chairs staring off into space. Uncle Paul shivered from the inside out. I had never seen such determination on a person's face. Slowly his eyes dried and cleared.

Uncle Paul was fighting another war and just like in Vietnam, he came back. Maybe he didn't come back as whole as when he left, but he came back.

"I love Nita," he said. "Maybe love her more than is likely healthy. I love that woman to the point of worship. And she loves me or loved me when she had all her mind. I know that. And loving, trusting a man was hard for her."

When Uncle Paul and Aunt Nita married it was the second marriage for both of them. I never knew anything about Uncle Paul's first marriage and there were only whispers about Aunt Nita's. But the whispers were not good.

Her first husband was an abusive drunk. Aunt Nita was young and in the 50's divorce was not a good, Christian option. She stuck it out until she was sent to the hospital one too many times.

"I've seen bad things. Things I cannot, things the man won't let me forget. But that's all right. When all is said and done, if all I've accomplished in this life was love that woman in there." He gestured with his beer hand back to the mobile home. "Spent a lifetime loving her the way she deserves to be loved. Well, I have fulfilled my purpose. Watching her die is hard but she is dying knowing she is loved. She may not know much else but she knows she is loved. I believe that. She will die knowing she is loved."

Uncle Paul looked at me and waited until I met his stare. "And I love you. I was there as much as I could be for you. I want you to know that."

"I know, Uncle Paul."

"It is important to me that you know that. It is also important you know about the man. He's still out there. I feel a connection somehow."

Uncle Paul continued to stare at me dead on. Searching my eyes for understanding and love. He found them, no problem.

"I think this is it. He shows you the past, the horrible parts of the past. And the thing is no one lives in the now. There is no now. You live constantly moving into the next moment, never knowing what comes next. I don't think anyone knows what comes next, not even the man. That is why he wants to make sure you remember the past because that's all he or anyone knows. He can't show you the future because there is no guaranteed future. The future just unfolds, and it just ends when it ends. Your only impact, the only part of you that carries on into the future is your past. What you have made and built with the time allotted."

Uncle Paul drained his beer in one long draw.

"I loved a woman. Pure and true. I loved you and tried to teach you what little usefulness I know. And maybe. Maybe by going back all those times to Vietnam, I at least extended a few more futures. I didn't save lives, you can't save lives because every life ends when it ends. But maybe, and that's the scary part, because maybe I didn't, but maybe I allowed a few lives to stretch on longer. Allowed them the opportunity to serve their purpose."

"If that is all I managed to do with my time, that is good enough for me. But there is one last thing. You need to believe the man is still out there. He looks for people like you. People with buried memories. You have to be aware of him. Know that and don't let him do to you what he did to me."

We didn't talk much after Uncle Paul told me about the man in Dick Van Dyke's hat. We drank a few more beers, I went and said goodbye to Aunt Nita and drove home.

Aunt Nita died a few months later. Uncle Paul followed almost a year after. The family said he died of loneliness and a broken heart. I knew better.

I spent a few years kicking around Fort Worth taking meaningless jobs and looking over my shoulder for the man. I felt his presences a few times. Once walking down Exchange Avenue on a Sunday morning I broke out in a cold sweat and my spine physically shivered. Another time, standing in front of the Caravan of Dreams smoking a cigarette, I almost thought I saw him. But he didn't show himself. If he was there at all.

I finally decided to live this way was bullshit. I went looking for the man. I soon learned you don't see the man, he sees you. So I searched for the broken souls who had seen his cotton candy. Turns out there are a lot of them and when you know what to look for, they are easy to find.

I've been on six of the seven continents. I've talked to bus drivers, actors, housemaids, presidents, poets and coalminers. I've heard a lot of horrifying stories. I don't think you can put the genie back in the bottle but a shared experience is a balm of sorts.

When the man in Dick Van Dyke's hat feels my presence in a place he leaves. He leaves before he is ready. That is my purpose.

TWAS THE NIGHT BEFORE, THE NIGHT BEFORE CHRISTMAS

By Kelley Baker

"Shit, is that Lou Reed?" I think to myself.

He steps out of the elevator with a blonde woman who's fighting her Social Security years by sporting one of the shortest dresses I've ever seen. The hair color is obviously not natural but those legs are impressive. Think Tina Turner. Her coat is some kind of fake animal thing, cut above the waist allowing plenty of space for everyone to take in her legs.

Lou is sporting shiny jet-black heavily dyed hair, small round dark glasses at night, and he's wearing a floor length hairy black coat. I'm not sure what kind of an animal it was supposed to be but it certainly looks better than his hair.

Then there are the old people. You hardly notice them dressed conservatively in overcoats for protection from the elements. They're easily in their late 80's.

They come off the elevator together and that's when Lou makes a beeline for the piano. The regular piano player is on break talking to friends and looking very dapper in his cheap Men's Wearhouse tuxedo. As dapper as one can look with a receding hairline and a potbelly.

Lou sits down at the piano and stretches his fingers. I'm hoping for *Sweet Jane*, or at least, *Walk On The Wild Side*?

Come to think of it, is the Blonde really a woman?

Blondie seat's the old couple at a table next to the piano. Maybe they're her parents? Maybe they're his? Can you imagine Lou Reed's parents?

Lou starts playing some classical piano piece and the parents are digging it, in a parental way, bobbing their heads to the music and smiling.

I'm sitting in the lobby of the Hollywood Roosevelt Hotel nursing a bourbon. I'm tired, I miss my kid, and I'm cold. And being cold in Los Angeles has got to be one of the most depressing things imaginable. There's ice forming on the streets tonight.

Sure it's December but this is the city where the sun shines all the time. When I lived here it was always warm in December. I used to call friends who lived up north just so I could ask them about their weather. Then I'd casually say that it was 80-something here and I'd just come back from the beach.

I was kind of a prick in those days.

I don't want to be here. I should be happy, but I'm too tired. I flew in this morning to screen an answer print of my first feature film, *Birddog*. Two years ago I finished doing the sound design on *Good Will Hunting* and then poured my heart and soul, along with all of my money, in to *Birddog*.

I also did the sound design on the remake of *Psycho*. People think I sold out but what I really did was make enough money to finish my film. I haven't had a break in two years and even though *Birddog* looks and sounds great I still need to market it and the next six months are going to be brutal.

I'm exhausted and lonely.

The waitress appears at my side. "Would you like another bourbon?"

"Thinking about it."

"You should give me your order now if you want one. It's going to be intermission shortly and it'll be a while before I can get back over here."

"Intermission?"

"There's a play in the theater. It's packed."

"Then I guess I better."

I love the Roosevelt because it makes no sense. I've been staying here off and on for years and I've never even seen the theater doors open let alone see anything going on inside.

One night I came back from a screening and decided to have a nightcap. I waited at the lobby bar for a couple minutes then finally called out towards the back.

"Hello. Anybody around?"

An exhausted forty year old wearing a white shirt, black vest and a two-day shadow appeared from somewhere.

"Can I get a drink?"

"We're closed."

"What time do you close?"

"Midnight."

I look at the clock on the wall. "It's only ten pm?"

"Yeah, but it's dead. So we're closed."

He turns and quickly disappears in to the darkness.

The Roosevelt's seen better days, which is part of its appeal. It was built in 1927 on Hollywood Blvd across from the Chinese theater. It's kind of seedy and the rooms are small, but it has this feeling of old Hollywood. Old seedy Hollywood. Old decrepit Hollywood. My kind of Hollywood.

The rooms are fairly cheap, parking is reasonable, and you can get around the city easily because of its central location.

A lot of bands and minor celebrities stay here. One time I was waiting for my car and an exhausted, make-up less Gwen Stefani and the rest of the band No Doubt came downstairs to get their van. I could see the hangovers in progress.

I overheard one of them say the previous night's show was a good one but the after-party went on forever. A few weeks later their record *Tragic Kingdom* came out. I'm pretty sure Gwen doesn't stay here anymore.

My drink arrives.

As Lou plays I'm watching a very skittish guy nervously circle the lobby looking for someone. I doubt he's staying here. He's dressed too shabbily even for this place in a worn Levi jacket, torn jeans, and acne scars. He grabs an old coffee cup someone left on a table. He takes a swig then realizes it's empty.

He walks over to the coffee stand and refills it with whatever dregs are left from the day. I count as he dumps ten packets of sugar in to it. Not the phony sugar either. The pure cane stuff. Mr. Coffee takes another lap around the lobby gulping this mixture down, then disappears out the back door.

Lou plays on. The Blonde beams, the parents nod to the music while Tuxedo Piano Guy continues to talk to a couple guys who've dropped by.

I think I'm getting a cold.

Tuxedo Piano Guy's friends are dressed to the nines and talking about a party happening later. They're trying to get him to join them. I hear one of the fellows use the term, "lotsa young cute guys there…" the rest is lost in Lou's piano as he switches tempo.

Across the lobby the side doors of the theater are thrown open and festively dressed people pour out in suits, long gowns, furs, and too much jewelry. It looks like a Christmas show crowd. The noise level in the lobby shoots up and competes with Lou's playing. The old couple turns and looks as the crowd stampedes towards the bar like a herd of thirsty steers coming upon a watering hole.

The bar isn't big and it's quickly engulfed in a sea of people shouting for attention. I watch my waitress shove people out of the way in a vain attempt to get to her station.

Mr. Coffee has returned, weaving in and out of the crowd with a too skinny guy in tow. Too Skinny looks worse than he does. Hanging on tightly to his cup Mr. Coffee makes his way back to the coffee stand. Grabbing another refill I watch as he adds another ten packets of sugar. Too Skinny is frantically searching for someone. Mr. Coffee offers the cup to his buddy who shakes his head in quick jerky motions as he continues to scan the over dressed crowd.

Lou decides he's done playing the piano for this new larger unappreciative audience. He and Blondie help the old couple up and push their way through the lobby crowd and out the front door. I'm left wondering what's next on their itinerary.

It dawns on me that the shabbily dressed guys are junkies as they continue making their way through the crowd in desperate search of someone. Mr. Coffee continues gulping down the mess in his cup.

Sitting at a high table on a stool by the bar I realize I'm pretty exposed. As the junkies move towards me I notice my drink change is sitting across from me. In a not so subtle way

I grab my cash and pull it close. They change direction and disappear out the door.

A voice shouts from across the lobby, "The play resumes in five minutes. FIVE MINUTES!"

It's an amusing site to see such a classy group chug their white wine and cocktails like a bunch of longshoreman.

Again the voice booms, "PLEASE RETURN TO YOUR SEATS. THE SHOW STARTS IN ONE MINUTE!

Like the outgoing tide the crowd quickly recedes back towards the theater. In just a few moments the doors close and the lobby returns to normal. Whatever normal is here.

It's not very late and even though I'm exhausted I know I'm not going to be able to sleep. It was a stupid idea to come down to Los Angeles this close to Christmas even if the print needed to be screened. I should have done it after the holiday.

What am I even thinking? I don't like holidays. Well Christmas is okay but only because my daughter is seven years old. I like how she loves Christmas. I realize there has been too much travel lately and too much time away from home. I close my eyes to let them rest for a moment.

"Do you have any requests?"

My eyes pop open and Tuxedo Piano Guy is standing at my table.

"Excuse me?"

"I take requests is there anything you'd like to hear?"

"Naaa. I'm good."

"Mind if I sit down?"

"Aren't you supposed to be playing?"

"I still have a few minutes."

He pulls out the other stool while I'm thinking this is the longest music break I've witnessed anywhere.

"So what brings you to LA?"

"A couple meetings. I'm headed out early tomorrow."

"Oh." He looks sad. Why the hell does he look sad? And why the hell is he talking to me?

"I've had a really long day. I started at noon playing at a mall in Sherman Oaks."

I nod. What else can I do?

"This is a busy time of year so I have to take advantage of it."

I nod again.

"I've been booked from the beginning of November through the first of the year. Sometimes two or three gigs a day"

"Tis the season for live piano music I guess." What the hell does that even mean?

"So what do you do?" Tuxedo Piano Guy asks.

"Like everyone else down here I'm in the film business."

"What floor are you staying on?"

I suddenly have a strange feeling.

"I'm really looking forward to getting home and spending time with my kid and my girlfriend tomorrow."

"The upper floors are nice and quiet. I've been in a few of the rooms up there."

The kid and girlfriend line didn't even slow him down. I notice Mr. Coffee and Too Skinny are back wandering around the lobby, checking all the corners. I change the subject.

"It must get expensive getting your tux dry-cleaned all the time? How often do you take it in?"

"Oh I have four of them so I can go quite a while and then have three of them cleaned at one time. It's really not a hassle."

"So was that Lou Reed playing earlier?"

"I don't know who that is."

"Velvet Underground? Take a Walk On the Wild Side? Sweet Jane? Heroin?"

He shakes his head.

The waitress appears. "Ready for another?" My glass is over half full.

The Tuxedo Piano Guy looks at me. I realize that besides me the only other people in the lobby are the two wandering junkies and I'm pretty sure they're not listening to him play.

I look at the waitress.

"Was that Lou Reed in here earlier playing the piano?"

"I didn't notice."

"Do you know if he's staying here?"

She shrugs.

"Even if you did know you couldn't tell me could you?"

She looks at Tuxedo Piano Guy.

"Aren't you supposed to be playing?"

"I'm just going back right now." He says as he slides off the stool.

She stands there for a moment waiting for him to leave.

"It's been nice talking to you." He extends his hand. I shake it.

"Yeah, you too."

"And if you have any requests…"

I say nothing so he heads back to the piano.

I turn to the waitress. "Thank you."

She smiles and is gone. I take a long slow drink.

I see Mr. Coffee plop down on one of the brown leather sofas clutching his cup like it's the Holy Grail. Too Skinny joins him. They stare at the front door.

Tuxedo Piano Guy starts playing some show tune from South Pacific. That's not very Christmasy.

In to the Lobby burst two very attractive young men and an older woman all dressed up for a night on the town.

They beeline straight to the piano and loudly squeal as they see Tuxedo Piano Guy. He stops, jumps up, and hugs the two guys. He's introduced to the woman and he dutifully shakes her hand.

They sit down at the table next to the piano, previously occupied by Lou Reed's parents, and start chatting excitedly as Tuxedo Piano Guy sits back on the bench and resumes playing. This time it sounds like some slow classical piece. He effortlessly has a conversation with them as he continues playing.

The waitress saunters over to their table to take drink orders.

The older woman orders drinks for all of them including Tuxedo Piano Guy as he continues to play. The two young men are talking and laughing too loudly. They appear to be in competition with the piano for volume. They are winning easily.

A conservatively dressed older man walks in to the lobby and as he walks past, Mr. Coffee and Too Skinny get up quickly and follow him out the back door.

Really? No way I would have pegged that guy as their connection.

My eyes are suddenly very tired. Maybe I'll be able to sleep. I need to be up by four a.m. if I want to shower and make it to the airport on time. Luckily the rental car drop-off is right at the airport so I can dump the car and go straight to the gate.

My drink is almost empty but I wait a few minutes before I kill it. I want to make sure Tuxedo Piano Guy is in the middle of a song because I have to pass right by him to get to the elevators.

I have a twenty-dollar bill in my hand as I empty the last of the bourbon from my glass and slide off my stool. I walk quickly to the piano drop the twenty in to his mostly empty tip jar and say, "Merry Christmas", never losing my stride. I'm at the elevator before he can even react.

As I step inside I feel good. Tuxedo Piano Guy is laughing with his friends, the Junkies have presumably scored, Lou Reed and his parents are off doing God knows what, and tomorrow I'll be home with my kid.

All is right in the world of the Roosevelt Hotel lobby.

Merry Christmas to all! And to all a good night.

LOCUSTS IN THE DISTANCE
By Mark A. Nobles

They found Tincy's body in a well in Watauga. They didn't find all of him but enough to know he wasn't eating chicken fried steak at Massey's or in a back room poker game somewhere on Thunder Road.

Tincy was a denizen of Jacksboro highway, an enforcer and extortionist who had, apparently, reached above his station or just plain pissed off the wrong people. Tincy was a bad man and to be considered a bad man on Jacksboro highway, well, you had to be one special kinda sombitch.

Detective Adair pulled up to the crime scene and stepped out of his unmarked car. He approached the Tarrant County ME, who was standing off to the side of the meat wagon. "Are we sure this is Tincy?" he asked.

The ME did not look up from his clipboard. It was 3am and he wanted to finish filling out his paperwork and get back to bed. "Since his face is splattered across the dirt and on the well, no, I can't state with 100 percent certainty that body was Tincy Eggleston, but," the ME paused to write more on the clipboard, "since no one has seen Tincy in almost three days and they found his car, abandoned and blood stained, two days ago, and his wallet and ID were in the jacket of the body pulled from the well, I'm pretty certain it's him. We'll run prints when we get the body back to the morgue."

"Head blown off, huh. Must have used a shotgun?" said Detective Adair.

"I guess that's why you're the detective," snarked the ME. He clipped his pen to the clipboard and placed it under his arm. "He was shot twice with double 0 buckshot. One to the back of the neck blew off his head except for his lower jaw and then, I guess they weren't certain the job was done, they put another, also point blank in his right side, below his armpit." The ME and Detective Adair watched the attendants load the body bag into the back of the coroner's wagon.

"Somebody wanted to send a message," said the detective.

"That would be my guess," said the ME. "And my message for you, detective, is I'm getting tired of scraping brains out of the dirt in the middle of the night up and down that god damn highway. I wish you boys would put a stop to this kind of shit." With that the ME walked away. He was not interested in Detective Adair's reply.

◆◆◆◆◆◆

The Major sat in his room at the Tower Motel, naked, drinking whiskey, chain smoking unfiltered Pall Malls, and staring at the wall. He had moved back to Fort Worth fourteen months prior. The siren song of LA had turned into a cacophony of brutal blows to the soul and crotch kicks to the ego, so he decided to limp back to the Fort he called home. When he moved away he was Alan Weaver, a young man headed to California in search of fame but he returned as Major Broiles, a tired and broken man wanting nothing more than to curl up and lick his wounds.

Fort Worth is a small city where it matters who your daddy is and from which side of the tracks you hail. He walked around town for four months waiting for someone to recognize him and call his 'Major' bluff. No one did, even people who had known him as Alan Weaver, just shook his hand and called him Major. The emotional scars and deep degradation LA had inflicted had evidently change him physically.

The Major soon realized this gave him an advantage. He knew Fort Worth, its players and layers, but Fort Worth did not know him. It was hard to hustle in Fort Worth as an outsider, but it wasn't impossible.

The Major had made a decent run in LA for a while as a low budget film producer, knocking out monster flicks, murder stories and the occasional stag movie when money got especially thin. With no film business to speak of in Fort Worth, he decided to reinvent himself as a West Coast music promoter and producer. Fort Worth had long been a hot bed of music talent. Milton Brown and Bob Wills had birthed Western Swing at Crystal Springs, and I.M. Terrell, the only high school in Tarrant County for coloreds, was turning out jazz musicians like Henry Ford turned out automobiles. The Major started booking bands and exotic dancers in the myriad of clubs lined up, butt to nut, along Jacksboro highway. He had to be careful, of course, as everything that drew money on Thunder road was controlled by old monied good ole boys and the mob. Fort Worth was and always had been a good ole boy town and nothing and nobody took a dime off the streets without three cents kicked back to the proper people. Fools and ignorants who thought they could muscle in or make a quick score were always sent packing to

Dallas with broken bones or missing digits, if they were lucky. Many simply disappeared into Lake Worth or down wells in Watauga or shallow graves in Saginaw.

··✦✦✦··

Which brings us back to Tincy and why the Major was sitting naked in his room, chugging whiskey, chain smoking cigarettes, and wiping vomit from the corner of his mouth. Tincy Eggleston was a gambler and racketeer who ran collections for a group of men best not named in print. When the Major started making the rounds attempting to book his acts on the highway, he started small, and asked nicely. Tincy let the Major book a few acts at an illegal gambling place owned by a giant of a man named Elmer Sharp. Elmer worked for gangster Asher Rome at the Black Cat Cafe but was allowed to hold poker games and sell rot gut hooch out of his garage. Until the Major started to bring in doo wop groups the only entertainment Elmer had was when he would occasionally wrestle a pet bear he kept chained in a corner. The Major quickly proved his worth matching talent to establishment and clientele and was given reign to book a few of the larger, slightly more upscale nightclubs.

Earlier that night the Major had been in the Black Sands, collecting pay for a burlesque headliner he had booked into the joint. After getting his cash from the owner he had gone to his car and discovered it would not start. Tincy, who had been inside exited into the parking lot as the Major stood with the hood open, cursing under his breath.

"Troubles?" asked Tincy.

"Apparently," replied the Major. "Drove up and everything was running fine, came out and it's dead as a doornail."

"Get in, I'll give you a ride, worry about it in the morning."

"Aces," said the Major.

Tincy climbed in behind the wheel of the Caddy and the Major opened the door to the front seat passenger side. "You still at the Tower?" inquired Tincy.

"Yeah."

"I have to stop by the Black Cat, won't be a minute, I'll drop you off after," said Tincy as he pulled out of the parking lot.

"Thanks."

"Why are you still at the Tower? Gotta be some bungalows around the lake that would be cheaper than paying weekly." said Tincy.

"Renting a house or bungalow would seem too much like putting down roots. I have an aversion to that," said the Major. "Besides, Rone cuts me a fair deal."

In less than five minutes they pulled into the parking lot of the Black Cat, a nightclub partly owned by Tincy. They had only passed one ambulance and two cherry tops in the eight block drive down Jacksboro. "Business is slow," remarked Tincy. Come on in for a night cap."

"Reckon I will," said the Major. In the two plus decades he had lived in California, the Major had completely lost all traces of his Texas accent and phraseology. He was surprised at how strong and how quickly it had resurfaced. In less than six weeks of being back in the friendly state the Major was full of 'howdy' greetings and always 'fixin to' do something.

The two men exited the long black caddy and crunched their way across the caliche parking lot. The Black Cat had been locked tight for the night but Tincy had key to the ready and the men entered and without locking the door behind them, headed straight to the bar. While the crime rate on Jacksboro was uncalculatable, most decent folks figured everything happening on the highway was a crime against God or man, no one would dare try and rob a joint as connected as Tincy's Black Cat. It would be akin to suicide. Tincy had no sooner filled two glasses with whiskey, the good stuff from under the bar, not behind it, then two men and a baby faced kid burst through the door.

Tincy did not flinch. "We're closed, boys. Head down the road."

"We're fixing to, you fat bastard, but you're coming with us," said baby face.

Tincy slammed the bottle on the bar for emphasis, "I don't think that likely." He said. "Unless you got at least two more friends with you meaner looking than these two palookas."

"Oh, we brought friends," said baby face. The other two men reached under their overcoats and each pulled out sawed off, double barrel shotguns.

"I'd keep those hands on the bar, lest my friends blow your head off right here and now." The baby faced kid walked up to the bar while the other two men came around from either end. The Major moved slowly away from the bar, making room for the kid.

"You boys are in for a world of hurt," said Tincy. "And it will all be for naught. I have a little scratch on me but the real money has been taken home for the night."

"Oh, hell, Tincy, this ain't a robbery, this here is an ass-sass-sin-nation," said the kid, grinning from ear to ear.

Quick as a lick, one of the men cracked Tincy in the side of the head with the butt of the shotgun. Tincy wobbled but did not fall down. The second man whacked Tincy in the face with the stock of his gun. The Major could see Tincy's eyes roll up into the top of his head. The two goons just stood and watched. After three beats Tincy collapsed. From where the Major stood on the other side of the bar it looked like Tincy took an elevator down. The kid giggled like a twelve year old.

"One, two, three, all fall down!" the kid clapped as he counted.

Oddly enough, the first thought the Major had when he heard Tincy hit the floor was how proud he was for not peeing his pants. One of the goons looked at the kid and motioned towards the Major. The kid let out a squeak and twirled around to face him.

"I almost forgot you were here," said the kid.

"I'd be glad to make like I was never in the room," said the Major.

"Oh but you are here," said the kid. "But you have behaved very well, so I will give you two choices, think carefully but answer immediately, because time is short. Ready? Good." The kid walked up to the Major, almost nose to nose. "Do you want to be a witness or an accomplice?"

Without blinking the Major replied, "Can I help move the body?"

The kid squealed again, "Good answer, good answer!" He then spun back around facing the bar. "Throw the rat bastard in his car, you drive, Crete and the rest of us will follow."

The Major walked around the bar and helped drag Tincy to the backseat of his car. He stirred once but another rap with the butt of the shotgun knocked him out cold. It also opened a gash in his forehead and the Major got blood all over his suit.

The two cars pulled up at the abandoned farmhouse on the outskirts of Watauga, three miles east of Saginaw. They kept the motors running and the headlights on bright. Tincy was limp as a bag of potatoes when they pulled him out of the back seat but when his heels hit the dirt he sprang to life and came up swinging.

The first goon never knew what hit him, more precisely, he never knew what bit him. He was dragging Tincy out of the back seat by the shoulders when Tincy reach up, grabbed him around the neck, pulled him down and bit his ear clean off. The goon screamed, dropped Tincy, stepped back and fell on his ass. He continued screaming, holding both hands over the hole in the side of his head where his ear used to be. There was a lot of blood.

Tincy leapt to his feet and turned to face the Major and the second goon, who were standing behind the backseat passenger door, waiting to each grab a leg after Tincy was pulled from the car. The Major was terrified and wondered how Tincy could see anything as his face was completely covered with sticky, half congealed blood from the gash in his forehead.

Tincy chewed the ear twice, then spit it directly in the face of the second goon. He let out a berserker bellow, charged the goon and put him in a bear hug. They grappled back and forth, then fell on the ground and began to roll around.

The kid, who had been doing blow in his car, finally got off, saw the commotion, grabbed the sawed off that had been sitting next to him in the car, and ran over. He waited, a bit impatiently, for Tincy to roll on top of the goon. When he saw his opportunity, he stepped up and stuck the shotgun just under Tincy's right armpit and squeezed off one barrel.

The blast sent a heavy mist of skin and blood everywhere. It also forcefully moved Tincy off the goon and on to his side, where he landed on his back. The compressed recoil broke the kid's wrist.

"Holy hell!" shouted the goon.

Tincy lay groaning on the ground. Slowly he rolled over on his left side and tried to stand. "I will kill you sons of bitches," he muttered. He was spitting blood and breathing heavily as he crouched on all fours, about five feet from the well.

"Finish off that asshole!" shouted the kid. The goon was now on his feet. The kid tossed the shotgun at the Major's feet, then grabbed his broken wrist and doubled over in pain. "Witness or accomplice, Major," he said. "Witness or accomplice."

The Major stood motionless. He was in complete shock. He had staged and filmed countless gangland murders for his films back in LA, but real life is much different than flickering shadows. The kid and the goon stared at him, waiting to see what he would do.

The Major couldn't believe Tincy had the strength to stand but was sure he would. There was only one shell in the sawed off. He briefly considered picking it up and blowing his own head off but he knew he couldn't. If he killed the kid, the goon would kill him and if he killed the goon, the kid would kill him. The only way for the Major to walk away from that farmhouse was to put Tincy down.

Tincy raised up on one knee and let out a piercing howl. The goon made a move for the shotgun but the Major beat him to it. He reached down, scooped it up, walked decisively over to Tincy, placed the barrel at the base of his skull and jerked the trigger.

Locusts. After the ringing in the Majors ears stopped, all he remembered hearing was the sound of locusts in the distance. The goon walked up, took the sawed off out of his hands and almost tenderly patted him on the shoulder. The goon walked over, placed the sawed off in the kid's car, walked back to the Major and they picked up and dumped Tincy, feet first, down the well. The Major got in the kid's car, the goon got behind the wheel of the caddy and they drove away from the farmhouse.

The kid dropped the Major on Jacksboro Highway in front of the Tower Motel wearing only his boxers and Undershirt. Before pulling away the kid reached in the backseat, grabbed a full bottle of whiskey and handed it to the Major. "Sorry to leave you like this, Major, but your clothes need to be burned. You know how it goes." The kid's left arm was hanging out the window. He slapped the car door twice with the palm of his hand. "Maybe we'll pick you up on the next job," the kid said with a grin. "Ya done good. Ya done good." The kid snorted, laughed, and sped away, spraying gravel like a banty rooster tail.

An hour later, the Major sat in his room, naked, chain smoking unfiltered Pall Malls. The whiskey bottle, half empty, rested on the nightstand.

The Major was doing his best to think about nothing. Nothing at all.

LITTLE BLACK DRESS
By Kelley Baker

"Who's the woman in the black dress?'
"That's the one I was telling you about."
"No way. Forget I asked."
"She's Alex's best friend. You guys would be perfect."

Thomas shakes his head. He wants no part of this. His divorce isn't final and yet all of his friends are constantly trying to set him up. The woman in the black dress is beautiful and totally out of his league.

"I'll introduce you two."

"No. Don't. If she's Alex's best friend and we start going out, if it doesn't work out then Alex will get pissed and you and I won't be able to hang anymore."

"What?"

"That's how it works."

"That's crazy."

"If I break up with her best friend, I'll be black balled."

"You're nuts."

Thomas doesn't want to be here. He only came because Mike's getting married and he's a good friend. Thomas conned another friend, Phil, into coming so he could use him as an excuse to leave early.

Phil's the wingman. Not as far as looking for women, but for getting Thomas out of here.

The wedding's outside of town at a winery so Thomas decides to drive his old '61 Austin Healey. It's one of the few things he enjoys these days. He fell in love with the Austin Healey when he was eighteen. He searched for over twenty years until he finally found one in decent shape and affordable, so he snapped it up. When he feels down he goes for long drives. The car isn't perfect, but when he's behind the wheel all of his cares dissolve. He's at one with the road and the universe.

He parks away from the others. He isn't afraid of anyone running in to it or scratching the paint. He wants to be able to make a clean escape.

Thomas and his soon to be ex-wife separated ten months ago. He was shocked when she told him she wasn't in love with him. She moved out and immediately moved in with another guy. Fifteen years gone. Thomas doesn't know what the future holds but right now he wants to be left alone.

But it's Mike's wedding so he shows up.

"Hey you made it!" Mike greets him at the door.

"I wouldn't miss this." Thomas says half-heartedly.

"I wanna introduce you guys to an old college buddy, this is Dave. Dave, this is Thomas and Phil. Dave's my best man."

Dave's handshake feels slimy and he's trying too hard to be firm.

Something catches Mike's attention. "Excuse me guys I need to say hello to Alex's work friend's. I'll be right back."

Mike walks off leaving Dave standing there with Thomas and Phil.

"So, you from around here?" Phil asks.

"No, I live in Frisco… Work for a big agency. Account exec. Just flew up for the weekend to be with my boy Mike!"

Thomas suddenly knows everything he needs to know about Dave.

"You guys checked out the bridesmaids yet?"

Thomas shakes his head.

"Well keep your hands off the maid of honor. She's mine."

Dave does one of those pistol things with his hand.

"We hung out last night. She's in to me. I'm gonna have a good time later."

Phil points to the open bar in the corner. Thomas nods and they head over with Dave at their heels.

"I don't know why he's bothering to marry her. I told him, just live with her. I've been living with the same woman for ten years. I don't need to get married." Dave says.

Thomas takes a huge swig of the beer he just grabbed. "It's going to be a long couple hours," he thinks to himself.

Mike appears and grabs Dave, "Come on man. We're gonna start."

Everyone forms a semi-circle as the music starts playing and Alex comes down the stairs with her maid of honor and bridesmaids. Thomas is happy the wedding is starting. The sooner they get married the sooner he can leave.

The ceremony comes to a screeching halt when the bride realizes she's misplaced the ring, which turns out to be a bad omen but that's another story. There's a little confusion and a friend of hers runs back upstairs to find it. When she comes back Thomas sees her gracefully move through the crowd all calm and cool with the ring. She places it in the bride's hand and then moves back into the group.

She's gorgeous in a little black dress. She has shoulder length reddish/brown hair, nice legs, and beautiful smile that stops him cold. She's a vision of loveliness.

Thomas assures himself she's not alone. Women like that don't come to these things by themselves. They always have dates.

With the ceremony finally over Phil drags Thomas to the buffet line. Thomas is quietly planning his escape after they eat.

After working the crowd Mike finally comes over.

"Congratulations man!" Thomas says as he hugs Mike.

They make small talk and that's when Thomas mentions the woman in the little black dress.

"She's here with a photographer buddy of mine, but I think they're just friends."

"We need to take off." Thomas says.

"No problem. Wait here for just a moment. I got something for you."

Thomas finds himself having meaningless conversations with people he barely knows. If Mike isn't back soon he's grabbing Phil and leaving. He'll apologize later.

"Hey man, I have someone I want you to meet."

Thomas turns and there's Mike and the woman in the little black dress.

"Thomas, this is Grace. Grace. Thomas. Thomas is one of my closest friends. I thought you guys might like to meet."

Grace is even more beautiful up close. She holds her hand out and Thomas shakes it. Then a funny thing happens. Everyone in the place disappears. In Thomas' mind all of the noise is gone and all he sees and hears is Grace.

She's smart, sarcastic, and focused solely on him. Thomas finds himself laughing which he hasn't done in a long time.

"Hey, how's it goin?"

Dave joins them and looks at Grace.

"I'm Dave. The best man."

"I know, I saw you during the ceremony."

"I saw you too." Dave says wolfishly.

Grace rolls her eyes.

"What's going on Dave?" Thomas asks.

"Nothing. Just preparing for a great night. The maid of honor and I are getting together after this."

Thomas says nothing. Dave gets the hint.

"Okay, I'll talk to you both later." Dave wanders off.

"What's that all about?" Grace asks.

"I haven't a clue."

Phil keeps checking in with Thomas, Thomas waves him off.

Time flies by and it's announced that the reception is ending. It's time to go.

Thomas isn't ready for this to end. He doesn't want to be involved with anyone but... Besides, isn't she here with someone else?

Dave comes running up.

"We're heading over to some blues bar that Sharon knows about. She's wondering if you guys want to ride with us?"

"I'm in if you're in." Thomas says to Grace.

"What about your car?"

"Phil can drive it home."

"Then I'm in too."

"Great I'll tell Sharon!" Dave runs off.

After a quick conversation with Phil, Thomas hands over his keys.

"I can't believe you're letting me take your car. You must really like this woman."

"I think so." Thomas says surprised. "Take care of it man. I'll call you tomorrow."

Thomas doesn't know what Grace told the photographer but the guy is glaring at him. He doesn't care.

They make their way out to the parking lot where Dave and Sharon wait. It isn't until they're driving down the road that Thomas realizes Sharon has zero interest in Dave.

But here he is in the back seat of a strange car with a woman he just met and she continues to make him laugh.

As they drive down the dark road she tells him to look out the window.

"It's dark. I can't see anything?"

"I know but I need to take my pantyhose off. It's driving me crazy. I don't want you watching."

It's cramped in the back seat of the econo box rental car. Thomas turns his shoulders towards the window wondering if he'll be able to see anything in the reflection. He can't. Her leg hits him in the back a couple times as she struggles to get her pantyhose off.

"There."

"Can I look now?"

"You can look. I'm just shoving this in to my purse."

Thomas has never met anyone like her. He still believes Grace is totally out of his league. He's had enough wine so he isn't nervous about this. It's just something he knows.

"I still can't believe you just gave your friend that cool car."

"I'd rather be here."

The blues bar is a madhouse. It's Saturday night and the place is packed. Thomas grabs two glasses of wine while Grace finds a small table in the corner where they can stand and talk.

Dave approaches him as Grace heads to the ladies room.

"Hey man, I need a favor?"

"If I can."

"I need you guys to take off."

"Excuse me?"

"Sharon really digs me and I feel like as long as you two are around it just complicates everything. If I have her to myself it's gonna be great."

"You are delusional, she has no interest in you." Thomas thinks.

"Let me talk to Grace and see what I can do." He says.

"Thanks man," Dave takes off looking for Sharon.

When Grace returns to the table Thomas fills her in.

"I just saw Sharon in the restroom. She hates that guy."

"I figured. So listen, I don't live that far from here. We can get a cab to take us to my house where I have another car and I can give you a ride home. All above board. I won't try anything, it's just I want to spend more time with you and I'm tired of all the noise here."

A few minutes later they find themselves in a cab heading for Thomas' house. He gives her a quick tour of his place including the little fountain in his backyard. He refers to his backyard as the fortress of solitude. It's where he likes to sit and listen to the water. It's here they kiss for the first time.

He drives her home and she invites him in for another glass of wine.

Sitting on her couch they talk. And they talk. And they talk.

"I hope your photographer friend isn't too pissed?" Thomas says not really meaning it.

"Who knows with him? I thought he wanted a relationship but I guess not, I'm not sure what he wants."

"So you guys aren't together?"

"No. He's freelance and I hire him to do work."

Thomas reaches over and kisses her again.

"Wow!"

Grace smiles.

"You know… I saw you from upstairs. When you were walking up to the building. I thought, there's a good-looking guy. Alex told me you and Mike were close friends."

He kisses her again.

"So how long have you and Dave been friends?"

"Dave and I are not friends. I just met him at the wedding."

"What?"

"I never saw him before today. Mike introduced me when I got there."

"You guys act like you've known each other forever?"

"Oh no! I don't think he knows anyone besides Mike. And I'm surprised he and Mike are friends. He's really obnoxious."

"Oh God I'm so glad to hear you say that."

"Yeah, I wonder how he and Sharon are working out?"

"He reached over and put his hand on her leg when we were at a stoplight. She kicked him!"

Thomas laughs. "Do you think she's gonna leave him at the bar?"

"I would." Grace says without hesitation.

"Ya know the bastard thing about that guy is he's been living with some woman for like ten years." Thomas shakes his head.

"He seems like that kind of guy."

"So you used to be married?" Thomas asks.

"Yeah. It didn't last long."

"Any kids?"

She shook her head. "You?"

"A three year old daughter. It's joint custody but she spends more time with me than her mother."

"I've never dated a guy with a kid."

"Me either." Thomas said. "But I'm not in to guys."

Grace laughs easily. He loves the way her smile lights up a room. He's feeling comfortable which of course makes him nervous.

"I'm not spending the night."

"I know you're not." Grace replies.

"I'm just trying to take all of this in."

"Me too."

"Can I see you again?" Thomas blurts out.

"Since you're not friends with Dave, I'll say yes."

"Okay, I won't ask when 'cause that'll seem a little psycho. In fact when I leave I won't call you for at least twenty-four hours so you'll think I'm normal. If you think that I'm normal that is?"

"You're leaving?" Grace looks at him.

"It's six am and it's getting light."

"What?" Grace reaches up and opens the curtain behind the couch.

"Wow. That happened fast."

"Yeah, I guess I did spend the night…" Thomas says with a grin.

There are two empty bottles of wine sitting on the coffee table and Thomas doesn't feel drunk or tired.

Less than twenty-four hours ago he was dreading going to a wedding and now he doesn't want to leave the house of this woman he just met.

He kisses her a few more times at the door then walks out to his car. Slowly he pulls out of her driveway as she watches him from the front window. She's smiling.

There is magic in meeting someone for the first time and knowing they're the one. Getting to know each other is fresh and exciting. The morning explodes with possibilities. As the sun rises, so do Thomas' spirits. Yesterday he was depressed. Today he's looking forward to whatever's next.

He'll be back. He knows it.

Now he has to call Phil and get his car.

Zade Teagarden sat on the park bench looking like an emaciated caricature of old man winter. He sat alone, on the far right side of the bench, looking as if he might be waiting for someone to join him. He was not. Zade Teagarden always sat alone, day after day, on that bench in that park.

He was a long man. Not tall but long. From his face to his fingers, from his body, and his legs, he was long. His dark blue overcoat swallowed him whole. His neck and hands extended from the coat openings as pale and bare as the leafless winter branches of the birches lining the path through the park. He didn't breath, he sighed, in constant succession. The squirrels, children, and joggers scurried, tumbled, and plodded by as the old man sat and watched.

Fall ended, and winter began. Winter, the season of long shadows.

Thursday afternoon was turning out to be the same as the first four days of the week, cold, dry and windless. Zade sat on his bench staring absently down the path to his right. He looked to be a thousand miles or possibly a thousand years away.

He rubbed his left knee with his left hand. The park was fairly deserted being mid-week and mid-winter.

Slowly down the path, approaching him was an even older looking woman. She moved with the assistance of an aluminum walker. She looked as if she could have been brushed over by a stout look, but she couldn't because Zade was shooting her his meanest and coldest and still she came.

The old woman paid no heed. She plodded, eyes on the path in front of her, with great deliberation, all her concentration focused on her next step or the next crack in the concrete. It took her twenty minutes to cover the last ten yards to the bench. Only when she finally reached the bench did she chance to look up.

"Good afternoon," she said to Zade. "It is a lovely day, isn't it?" Her voice was smooth and clear, the voice of a much younger woman.

Zade answered with silence and for the first time in fifteen minutes looked away from the woman and gazed back down the path. It took her a few minutes to turn herself around and sit on the bench.

"May I share this bench with you for a short while?" she said. "My name is Mrs. Cleasedale," she paused, then repeated, "Mrs. Cleasedale." After another pause, she continued, "Formal names are so nice, don't you think?"

Zade ignored her and continued to stare into the distance and rub his knee.

"It gives a person dignity, identity, to be called by their last name. Don't you think?" She pulled her walker closer to her, and it banged the bench. Zade turned and glared at her but said nothing. Mrs. Cleasedale, her every move difficult and deliberate, looked ahead, her eyes clear and bright. She did not notice his glare.

"At Crested Manor, that's where I live, do you know it? It's on Twelfth Avenue, off Rosedale. Anyway, they call you by your first name there, like you were a child." Then in a much higher voice than her own, she said, "Claire, oh Claire, what would we like to eat today. Claire, you chew your meat good now." She waved a finger in front of her nose. Then, in her natural voice, and with a thick slab of indignation, "I am Mrs. Cleasedale. I'm eighty-three years old, and I damn well know how to chew meat." She giggled, turned and directly addressed Zade for the first time. "They treat me like a child, Mr." She stopped for a moment. "I'm sorry, I haven't given you a chance to even introduce yourself. Mr.?"

"Zade," he replied. His voice was hoarse and phlegmy and his tone sounded as if it was the end of the conversation.

"Mr. Zade," she rolled the name off her tongue. "What an unusual surname."

"It is my Christian name," he said as he looked away. This definitely was the end of the conversation.

A look of embarrassment and perturbation crossed Mrs. Cleasedale's face. Knowing when she is not wanted, she struggled to regain her feet behind the walker. Halfway up she lost her balance and the walker again banged the bench. Zade gave a disgusted sigh and made a quick, slight turn from her. Thirty minutes later he was again alone on his bench. He stared intently ahead as if he were watching a play.

The sound of boots treading dead leaves came from behind the bench. They sounded close but had not begun by sounding far away. A man turned the far corner of the bench as Zade turned to look. His overcoat still faced forward because it did not touch him in any discernable place one could see. The new man sat down on the far left corner of the bench. He looked about the same age as Zade. He was round with a bright pink tint to his skin. He had a smile on his face that made him look extremely pleased with himself.

"Hello, Zade," said the man on the left. He called the name in a familiar tone that disconcerted Zade.

"How do you know my name? I don't believe we have ever met." The last sentence sounded like a lie because Zade had the feeling he did know the other man.

"You know me, Zade Teagarden, you haven't seen me for a while, but you know me. I have been forgotten, but you know me well," said the man. He laughed a high-pitched laugh. Zade's eyes froze on the old man's face. He recognized the laugh; it involuntarily sent a cold chill up his spine. The memory rose in his mind from a long ago childhood.

◆◆◆◆◆

Zade was nine years old. He was standing in the middle of the toy aisle in front of the matchbox cars. His best friend, Jim Blight, was talking to him. "Come on, it's the neatest one in the collection, and you don't have it."

"But I don't have any money," said Zade in a pitiful voice.

"Just stick it in your back pocket and walk out," replied Jim. "Old Mr. Holster will never know. Come on!"

Zade had no chance to think or say anything because Jim stuck the red roadster into his back pocket and shoved him down the aisle towards the front door. Zade walked past the counter without looking at Mr. Holster behind the cash register. He felt like there was a siren going off in his head.

"Zade," said Mr. Holster, "what is that sticking out of your pocket?" Zade reached around and felt the front wheels and half the toy car sticking out the top of his left back pocket. He started crying almost at once and when he turned around, Jim was nowhere to be seen. Jim had gotten Zade in trouble again. Jim was always around for the planning but never around for the punishment. As Zade stood there in his embarrassment while Mr. Holster called his parents, he could hear, somewhere on the next aisle over, Jim's high pitched laugh. Zade's embarrassment and fear of the impending punishment faded and was replaced with hatred. A hatred that would grow throughout a lifetime and encompass more than just a nine-year-old prankster.

* * *

"Ahh, Zade, why don't we go for a walk? It is such a nice day." Said the old man with the pinkish face sitting on the left side of the bench.

"I don't like walks," said Zade emphatically.

"Oh poodles, man, you don't like anything. Why do you always just come out here and sit? We could have some fun."

Zade's eyes were wide with astonishment. He hadn't heard that expression in years.

"Oh poodles, man," he whispered.

* * *

The night was moonless and Zade couldn't see a thing. It was doubly dark in the back seat of the car, and his hot breath made it even more humid than it already was. He was sweating freely. Too freely he imagined. He knew even though it was dark, she could see. Ruth had big, cat-green eyes and Zade knew she could see in the dark.

"Oh, poodles, man," she had said not two hours before, "why not?" Ruth had finally decided to end her long and teasingly famous career as a virgin. Zade had been in the right place at the right time, that being a time when Ruth's boyfriend, Bob Daring, was not around. He was home sick with mono and had missed two weeks of school. So now Zade found himself wrestling with Ruth in the backseat of his father's Desoto, trying to touch and pull the right things, and he couldn't even see the damn things.

She lay there in the dark, her green eyes looking over and down into the floorboard. "Oh, poodles, man," she said again, this time she sounded bored.

"Where was that snap?" Zade thought as he pawed in clammy desperation.

After thirty-five minutes and not much progress, Ruth made a suggestion, "Why don't we just undress ourselves. You can undress yourself, can't you?"

Her sarcasm stung Zade's pride. He was losing face and that would not do in a situation like this, after all, he was the deflowerer.

He sarcastically replied, "Usually." However, it fell from his lips a pitiful statement. Ruth giggled.

"Excuse me. I'm going to step outside and catch some fresh air. Please be ready when I get back." He tried to make the last sentence sound forceful. It would have too if his voice hadn't cracked.

He stepped out of the Desoto and walked a few feet back down the dirt road. He was nervous and now had to go to the bathroom. There was a large pecan tree fifteen yards back of the car on the other side of the ditch. He stepped with his left foot to cross the three-foot deep ditch and the gravel gave way. His leg slid, and his knee twisted as he did the splits half in and half out of the ditch. He felt and heard his knee dislocate. It popped like a dud firecracker.

Ruth drove him to the hospital. Zade was screaming and crying so loud that in her hurry to put her clothes back on, she neglected to put on her bra. Naturally, the story of a braless Ruth, driving Zade to the emergency room at 1:30 in the morning, was told and retold all over town.

Bob Daring heard about braless Ruth. Three weeks later, after Zade was allowed to get around on crutches, Bob broke his nose. Zade couldn't walk without a limp or breathe through his nose for six months. His knee never fully recovered. It was stiff and numb for the rest of his life.

⸻ ⋆⋆◆◆⋆⋆ ⸻

Zade stared at the man across the bench with a look of hatred, pain and a little embarrassment. He didn't know who this man was, but he began to realize what he was doing.

He did not like it.

"Who are you?" Zade shouted, waving an arm and glaring at the pinkish man. "Who are you? How do you know so much about me? Why do you remind me of so much?" He turned away from the other man and stared in front of him. He slowly beat his left leg with his hand.

"Nobody could know these things. Nobody," he whispered. After a brief second of silence, Zade slowly turned and faced the other man, looking him straight in the eyes.

"Maybe I'm asking the wrong question." Then, in a low voice, "Maybe I shouldn't ask who are you, but, what are you."

The old man with the round, pink face only smiled. "I already told you, Zade. You know me."

"What are you? Why do you haunt me?" The other old man remained mute. "You think I'm wasting my life?" Zade continued. "You think I'm a sour old man rotting away, while life marches down this path? Well, I used to play, I used to play well. I got up every morning and I worked, and I scratched and I fought and I got kicked and I kicked back. But one morning I got up and my spirit, like my leg, was crippled and numb." Zade found himself out of breath as if he had been running, so he paused to regain it. His fist ceased beating his leg and went back to rubbing.

"So I stopped kicking." Zade turned and stared down at his knee. He was silent for a long while. "And the world never missed a step. It went right on without me." He paused. "It didn't even stop to claim victory."

Zade turned and looked the opposite way down the path. The way the old lady had gone. No one had passed since she left.

"Excuse me," said Zade. "You can have this fucking bench."

He stood and walked off down the path in the direction taken by Mrs. Cleasedale. It wouldn't take him five minutes to catch her. The afternoon grew late and the shadows long, finally overtaking the empty bench.

AT LEAST HE'S NOT A DRUMMER

By Kelley Baker

The ringing phone jolted Hank awake. He'd fallen asleep in the chair again.

Late night calls always make Hank nervous. They're never good news. He thinks about not answering but what's the point? They'll either leave a message, which he'll have to hear or they won't and he'll worry all night. He kicks himself for the thousandth time wishing he had paid the extra $1.50 a month for caller ID.

"Hello?"

"Hey Hank it's Denise. I hope I'm not calling too late?"

"You? Never. Is everything okay?"

"Yeah. Everything's okay…"

Her voice trails off.

Hank was working in LA when he met Denise. It was during one of his dark moods, where he felt the world closing in on him. Living in a hotel for six weeks can do that.

Hank decides a late night drive will help him sleep. Driving always calms him. Sometimes he'll drive all night trying to outrun his moods.

He drives aimlessly for a couple hours then spies a huge sign with the words, *21 Beautiful Women and 3 Ugly Ones.*

"What the hell…" he thinks pulling in to the semi-empty parking lot. The women who work Mondays may not be as beautiful as the ones who work weekends but they're always nicer.

"One drink then back to the hotel." He thinks to himself.

The music blasts as he walks in the front door. The bouncer looks at him semi uninterested.

"No cover. Two drink minimum."

Hank nods. The place is practically empty.

A short tattooed redhead works the pole for three guys sitting at the rack. She isn't really dancing mostly she's talking to the guys. She's more interested in their money than dancing.

The guys are drunk enough they aren't complaining. Between the three of them there's easily a-hundred-fifty bucks laying on the stage. They have that confident look like one of them is going to "get lucky". They won't. Hank's seen this play out a thousand times in bars all over the country.

Hank orders a drink and as is the practice with a two-drink minimum the waitress returns with two. Not that Hank wants two drinks but the waitress is going to make sure she gets all the money up front in case Hank decides to bolt after the first one.

After one drink you might leave if the place is slow. After two drinks, you'll probably order a third cause that's what the alcohol tells you to do. It's an old trick and effective.

As the song ends, Hank watches the red head pick one lucky guy and he follows her to a back area where he's going to drop a lot more money on private dances and still go home alone. His buddies are dejected, but they'll go home with fatter wallets unless another enterprising dancer gets to them first.

"Mind if I join you?"

Hank looks up. A dark haired woman is standing next to his table. She's dressed in a black slip that's sexy as hell because it leaves room for one's imagination.

"I'm not staying long."

"That's fine. It's slow and the manager wants us all out here. I'm Denise."

"Hank."

"So do you live around here?"

Hank shakes his head. "Down here for work. Staying in a hotel. Couldn't sleep, thought I'd take a drive and ended up here. I'll be heading back to the hotel after this. Got an early day tomorrow."

"Yeah, I've got a day job too. I dance two nights a week, the extra money's good."

Hank nods. She's sure he doesn't believe her.

The waitress appears and asks Hank if he wants to buy Denise a drink? It's the price you pay for having someone sit with you. He figures she'll order Champaign or something exotic and expensive.

"It's late. I'll just have a glass of the house white."

The waitress glares at Denise. This is not what she's expecting. She quickly leaves.

They make small talk. The waitress returns and puts the wine down, hard.

"That'll be twelve dollars."

This is the cheapest drink Hank has ever bought in a place like this. He hands her a ten and a five and waves her away.

"Thanks." She says, not meaning it, as she disappears.

Denise leans in.

"Listen, I'm probably going to get in trouble for not ordering something more expensive. A private dance would go a long way in their eyes."

"How much?"

"Twenty a song."

Hank holds up his drink.

"Let me finish at least one of these so I don't look like a crazy guy walking to the back with a drink in each hand."

Denise smiles.

Hank has a couple weeks of per diem he hasn't spent so it's not about the money, besides he's smart enough to have left most of it back at the hotel.

He finishes his drink as the next song ends so they make their way to the private area. Hank follows Denise down a long hallway to a small room. Inside it's the size of an office cubicle with a loveseat. There's no door, only a curtain that Denise pulls closed.

Hank sits on the loveseat and puts his drink down by his feet. Denise sits next to him.

"We'll wait for the next song so you'll get your twenty dollars worth."

"That's fine. I'm just happy to be where I can actually hear you."

They stay for half a dozen songs. Some songs Denise dances, others they talk. Hank's good at getting people to open up and before she knows it she's telling him her life story.

Denise is her middle name and she had a baby at eighteen. The guy promptly took off and she hasn't seen him since. It was just her and a new baby. She had no real skills, so she started dancing.

She took the money she made and put herself through school. She's a legal assistant for a big law firm. Even though she no longer needs the money she likes dancing two nights a week. The partners at the law firm have no idea.

Denise makes sure she's standing and dancing for Hank when the manager walks through and opens the curtain a little to make sure nothing "illegal" is going on.

Looking at Denise, Hank realizes she's older than most dancers. He guesses mid-forties. She has a few lines around her eyes but it's her hands that give her away. He also guesses correctly that her hair is dyed even if the drapes matched the carpet.

While Denise goes to the disc jockey to get out of her next dance shift, Hank walks out to the bar, gets another drink, and returns to the small room.

Hank pays for a couple more dances then it's time to go. He's tired and his mood has lifted.

"I work again on Thursday if you're interested?"

Hank nods but is non-committal…

"So how's work at the law firm?"

"It's good. They're keeping me busy."

"And your son?"

"He just got a nice promotion and is planning on coming out to spend Christmas with me. I'm pretty excited."

"That's great."

"Are you gonna be coming down here anytime soon?"

"I'm booked up here for the next month, after that I'm not sure." Hank says.

There's an awkward silence.

"I think we need to talk."

Oh Christ here it comes Hank thinks.

⁘⁘⁘

Hank goes back to the club on Thursday to see her.

The lights are flashing, the music's blaring, and there's a talkative DJ. All the things he hates.

Hank scans the crowd. It's too dark and too crowded so he finds a table, orders his two drinks and waits. He waves off two young and hungry dancers that approach him. Hank knows the rules. If you're sitting with a dancer the others have to stay away. He keeps the table open just in case.

As the next song starts he sees Denise up on stage. He watches to see if anyone moves up to the rack from a table and sits down. That usually indicates a dancer has been talking to someone. No one does.

He doesn't want to lose his table by moving to the rack so he sits back and watches. She's smart. After each song she pulls the money off the rack and on to the dance floor. After the third song she bends over and picks up the cash slowly to the delight of the guys sitting there.

Ten minutes later she stands next to his table.

"I wasn't sure I'd see you again. How's work?"

"Long day, but it's fine."

Denise sits and in no time a waitress appears. Denise orders a white wine.

"Could I get a dance in a bit?"

Hank doesn't want a dance as much as he wants to be in a quieter place. After a day in the studio his hearing's shot and he has two more days this week before he gets a break.

Hank stays for three private dances.

"I need to get outta here. The noise is killing me."

"Hang on a second."

As the next song starts Denise reaches in to her purse and hands Hank a card.

She whispers in his ear. "This is my cell. Call me if you'd like and maybe we can have dinner this weekend. My treat."

She kisses him on the cheek and walks with him to the front of the club.

By the time Hank gets to her place on Saturday it's eight o'clock. She surprises him with dinner already made.

"I figure you've been living in a hotel for so long maybe you'd like a home cooked meal."

They get together five more times before he spends the night and that's okay with both of them.

The more time they spend together the more comfortable he gets and his dark moods don't come as often. He no longer sees her at the club because she's working and he doesn't want to interfere. She's fine with that.

The job finishes and Hank goes home but is back a couple weeks later for another month. He has a day off mid-week so he goes by the law firm and takes her to lunch. They spend the weekend in a small town on the coast.

There's something deeply embedded in him that doesn't allow him to believe anyone would want to spend time with him. He tries to let go of those feelings but more often than not they creep around in his head. Denise never pushes him for any sort of commitment.

Often he goes to her place. She cooks dinner, he cleans up, and she's fast a sleep on the couch by the time he's finished. Hank lies on the couch with her. During the week he drives back to the hotel.

Over the next six months he isn't in LA at all. They talk a couple times a week and he keeps looking for reasons to see her.

When work dries up, like it often does, Denise offers to fly him down for a week but he feels funny having her pay for his ticket.

They talk on the phone less and less. Hank feels guilty about not going to see her. He keeps telling himself he can't afford it.

••••••••

"What do we need to talk about?" Hank asks.

The silence hangs in the air.

"I met someone…"

"That's fantastic!"

"What?"

"I said that's fantastic. Do you really like him?"

"Yeah, I do." Denise sounds confused.

"Listen I think it's great you found someone you really like."

"You do?"

"Listen, I'm not down there much and I have a bunch of commitments here and really, when it comes down to it, I want you to be happy. If that's with me or someone else it doesn't matter. The important thing is that you're happy."

Hank suddenly thinks, "Am I sounding too happy about this?"

"This isn't exactly what I expected." Denise says.

"Me either. You're fantastic and right now I can't be there for you and that bothers me. But if this other guy can…"

Denise is having a tough time wrapping her head around this.

"Are you seeing someone?"

"No. Just trying to find work and spend time with my kid." Says Hank.

"You're sure?"

"I'm sure."

There's another long pause.

"So what does this guy do if I may ask?"

"He's a musician."

"That's cool. What does he play?"

"He plays keyboards and does lots of session work. Hank, you know how I feel about you. We have so much fun and you're a great guy."

"Thanks. You're pretty terrific as well."

"But you don't live here."

"I know. I can't. I've done it. And that's not fair to you."

"And let's face it, you're not the most stable person in the world…"

"Excuse me?"

"You're not very stable. And that's what I really need right now. Stability."

"I … uh … Okay." It's Hanks turn to be confused.

"Brian is much more stable and he's able to give me what I need. And you can't."

"Cause I'm not stable…" Hank isn't sure where to take this.

"Right! Listen you're a great guy and I hope you finally work your stuff out."

"Work my stuff out?"

"You know what I mean."

More silence.

"Listen Hank, I need to go. You take care okay?"

"Yeah, you too. ... And congratulations on this new guy. I'm glad he makes you happy."

"Good night Hank."

"Good night."

Hank hangs up the phone.

"Shit. I just got dumped by an exotic dancer ... for a musician ... because he's more stable than I am? ... Let that sink in Hank..."

Hank sits quietly. He thinks about his life. His work. His moods. Should he call her back? Should he fly down to see her, maybe they can work this out?

Finally he rises from the chair to go to bed.

"Well, at least he's not a drummer. That would hurt."

THE CAT HAD BEEN CALICO

By Mark A. Nobles

Lamb stood at the intersection of Farm to Market roads 1008 and 24 chain smoking Pall Malls and repeatedly whistling the one-note guitar solo from 'Cinnamon Girl.' She stood motionless on the northeast corner of the crossroad, three empty cigarette packs, and 63 smashed butts scattered about her feet. Lamb had been waiting a while.

She had spent the last forty-two days walking the three hundred and ninety-six miles from her apartment in Fort Worth to the desolate intersection fifteen miles northwest of Muleshoe. For five full weeks Lamb walked sundown to sunup partially because it was cooler, but mainly by traveling after dark and sticking to the shadows she could avoid the meth-fueled truckers who almost always tugged their air horns as they passed and sometimes pulled over to offer unwanted and unsolicited rides. Most of the time the assholes were not talking about a lift to the next town.

Two days west of Sweetwater and two hundred and sixteen miles into the trip, Lamb quit removing her boots in the mornings. Her feet were so swollen she knew she would never get them back on if she ever took them off. At times she thought she would never make it to Muleshoe, but she did. Lamb had seen only one vehicle since turning onto FM 1008 for the final leg of her journey. A beat-up white Econoline van with midnight black tinted windows had come within inches of running her down only five miles from her destination. The van had come barreling along, half on the shoulder, at a high rate of speed, and almost clipped her before she jumped, tucked, and rolled off the asphalt and down to the bar ditch. Lamb never heard the van approaching. She only became aware she was about to be roadkill when the Econoline's headlights bathed her in that eerie blue halogen light and threw her own shadow before her.

The air was so still that the gray haze of the cigarette smoke hung around Lamb like tension at Thanksgiving when drunk uncle Ed starts talking politics at the table. At the stroke of midnight, Lamb bent down and rummaged through her backpack. Pulling out a sack of salt she struggled to get it open because her fingernails were trimmed past the quick. Once open, Lamb began wildly shaking the bag in all directions, spraying salt like confetti. Once empty, she bent down and rifled through the backpack again. One by one she pulled out three black cat bones, two femurs, and a rib. The bones were black, the cat had been calico. She tossed one femur over her left shoulder, dropped the other at her feet, then closed her eyes and tossed the rib straight up in the air. When the rib failed to fall back to earth, Lamb relaxed, opened her eyes, pulled the Pall Malls from her jacket pocket, withdrew one, lit it, inhaled deeply, and went back to waiting.

The still air grew heavy. The stars overhead did not twinkle, they shone steadily. The bats, flying high above Lamb feasting on mosquitoes, and occasionally dodging the odd flying cat rib, heard the slow approach of the Lincoln Continental nine minutes before Lamb. Slowly the sound of white wall tires rolling on asphalt could be heard by Lamb's frail human ears. She did not turn or in any way acknowledge the approach of the coal-black 1964 Lincoln Continental as it slowly rolled to a halt eighteen feet away from where she stood.

The back passenger suicide door opened and a tall, thin man stepped out of the Lincoln Continental. He had no outstanding features save a pencil thin mustache. His clothes were black and for a splash of color, he wore a lavender beret rakishly tilted atop his head. If the man had theme music, it would have been written and performed by ZZ Top circa 1978, but he did not have theme music because this was life, not a movie, so the night remained awkwardly silent.

Leaving open the suicide door the man made his way to the front of the Lincoln Continental, planted himself firmly, feet shoulder width apart, with his hands clasped at his waist.

The man and Lamb stood in silence for three minutes.

You called me? His words sounded thin and danced through the heavy air.

Lamb turned to face him but did not look him in the eyes. "I'm here to strike a bargain if the price is right and the return is fair weighted."

The price is non-negotiable, and I always deliver as promised.

"As I understand the transaction, you grant me wealth and fame in exchange for my soul." Her voice was steady, but Lamb was not metaphorically shaking in her boots.

Before we jump to the nitty-gritty, tell me just who am I dealing with?

"You don't know who I am?"

Oddly enough, I do not know who you are. When I am summoned, there's no caller I.D.

"I'm Lamb."

Just Lamb?

"Just Lamb."

Fair enough, Lamb. You may call me Hoof.

"Hoof?"

Hoof smiled and nodded.

This time.

"Fine. Whatever. We're not here for niceties, we're here to strike a bargain."

But niceties make it so much more pleasant.

"Can we please cut to the chase? I give you my soul and in return, my paintings will sell, for a lot of money, and I will gain a worldwide reputation as an artist. That is the bargain. Correct?"

Well…

"What the hell, Hoof, if that is your name, why would I sell my soul except for wealth and fame?"

No reason. Absolutely no reason at all to sell your soul except for wealth and fame, and many would argue even at that price it's a sucker's play.

"You really aren't a good salesman."

Don't need to be.

"So, spill it. What's the catch?"

No catch, but there are rules.

"Rules?"

Sure. Let me pose a question to you, Lamb. Can you paint my portrait, right here and now?

"If I had a canvas, brushes, and a palette I could."

So, you can't make your art without tools?

"Of course not."

Well, same holds true for old Hoof. I can't do what I do, which is make you famous and successful, without certain tools. One of those tools being the subject, in this case you, have to have at least a modicum of talent.

"I have talent. I just can't catch a break."

Of course. Happens every time and that's where I come in. I provide the breaks. I can make it so the right people become aware of your work. I can even make it so they are inclined to view your work favorably, but, and this is a big but, I can't make them say, let alone, think your work is great, timeless, or groundbreaking, if, in truth, your work is shit.

"Then what good are you? I may as well keep knocking on doors myself."

You could do that, but the doors would never open.

"Artists get discovered all the time."

My artists get discovered. No one gets a break except through me.

"I'm calling bullshit."

It's true. Every artist, in any discipline, that has ever, in the history of humankind, broken through to any modicum of success, has first made a bargain with old Hoof.

"Every single one."

You heard right.

"Michelangelo?"

Oh yeah.

A dreamlike countenance came across Hoof's face as he fondly harkened to Michelangelo.

Little known fact; Michelangelo was an extremely picky eater. Imagine, living in Italy, and only eating boiled meat and potatoes. Crazy, right?

Lamb is not interested in Michelangelo's eating habits. "It's just… I have trouble believing that every single artist ever…"

Hoof shrugged his shoulders.

"What about God? Surely, God has exalted artists that create great works in his name?"

Let me stop you down for a second and then I will address your question. Get this straight, God does not like it when people use pronouns in referring to God. God just likes to be called God. God is neither he nor she nor it. God is God. And as to your question, God doesn't work that way. I will repeat myself one last time. Every successful artist, even those praising God, became successful by signing on the dotted line with me. Every. Single. One. Ever.

"I still find that hard to believe."

Don't give a hoot what you believe. I know. And here's another tidbit. I'm not talking only painters, such as yourself, or writers, musicians, and the like. I once bargained for the soul of a guy who could fold pizza boxes like nobody's business. He was the best pizza box folder who ever lived. Before coming to me he was just toiling away, getting by, known as a really good employee who could fold boxes really fast, but, you know the drill, he was only making a living, nothing more. But man, could he fold pizza boxes. Developed his own method. Well, we struck a bargain and after that, he won a world championship in pizza box folding.

"There is such a thing?"

There is. He set the world record for folding pizza boxes, and now he owns his own pizza franchises, he was given a patent for his pizza box folding method, and was even featured in a national television commercial. People know his name. He has money. He's living the good life.

"And he folds pizza boxes… And you made him rich and famous."

He did things no one had ever done before. He was a creator. He had a skill and honed it to an art. That makes him an artist in my book.

"So, getting back to God. Are you telling me God could not make me successful?"

Oh, hell no. Listen to me, I said God doesn't work that way. Of course, God could make you wealthy and famous with a mere thought. Wildly, crazy successful, God is God. God can do anything God wishes. God simply chooses not to. God is more concerned with a person's unity and inner peace and one on one relationship with God and the universe.

"That doesn't make sense to me."

Do not waste your time cyphering out God's reasoning. It will get you nowhere, believe me.

"So, can you…"

No.

"But I didn't ask you my question."

But I know what's coming, it always comes, and the answer is no, I cannot tell how much talent you have or how much fame and success you will achieve if you make a bargain with me.

"Cannot tell or will not tell."

Cannot. Truthfully, I cannot. I just met you sugar, how in blazes do I know how talented you are?

"I have some pictures of my work on my phone, or if you have a hotspot in your Lincoln, I can show you my website. There's no damn service out here."

Hoof waves her off.

I am no judge of human artistic abilities. Hell, I thought Picasso was a no talent poser and George Clacker was going to set the world afire.

"Who's George Clacker?"

My point.

Lamb nodded.

Sometimes people are piss poor judges of their own talent. They are either imitators, not creators, or they are simply, atrociously, horribly bad at their chosen endeavor. If that is indeed the case with you, well…

"So, it is possible I could sell my soul and nothing changes. Nothing happens. I get nothing in return for my soul. I just continue to rot in obscurity, painting my paintings that no one sees, let alone buys."

Is it rotting? Really?

"It is rotting, really. I've been rotting my whole life."

How do you feel when you visualize the painting on a blank canvas.

"Like I have to pull it out. I have to fill the canvas with what I see in my head."

How do you feel when you finish a painting?

"That is the only time I feel complete. Like I have a purpose. Like I'm worth more than a littler shit."

And the painting exists, right? It is in the universe. It is a part of…

Hoof motions all around him and gazes up at the Milky Way.

"I've heard all that art for art's sake crap, and I ain't buying it. If a tree falls in the woods, does it make a sound?"

Oh, yes, it definitely makes a sound.

"But if nobody hears it, what's the point?"

The other trees hear it. The dirt hears it and feels it. The sky hears it. It is part of the universe and the universe knows the tree and that it has fallen.

"You are so full of shit."

I get that a lot.

"What's to stop you from taking my soul, doing nothing at all to help me, then, when I complain, you just say, (mocking Hoof's speech pattern) 'Sorry, sugar, I guess you're just a no talent piece of shit.'"

First of all, I told you I am no judge of talent, so I would never call you a 'no talent' and second of all, I told you, there are rules. That is not how this works, I always keep my end of the bargain. Always.

Lamb stares at Hoof but still does not look him in the eye. She's mulling him over.

Let me ask you this. What do you really want? Do you want fame and fortune? A stack of money, yea high.

Hoof raises his hand far above his head, thirty feet above his head, to be precise.

And do you want your work to hang in high toned galleries and important museums? Because if that is what you want, I'm your guy."

Hoof pauses.

Or, do you want to have your name listed and counted as one of the great artists of your generation, or hell, maybe even all time?

"I don't know. Maybe both."

Fair enough. But let me tell you this, you cannot imagine the art created in what you call obscurity, that no one, save the creators themselves, God, and the universe, have seen. Some of this art is so beautiful God wept when it was created.

"That sounds a little hyperbolic."

I have it on good account as true.

"So, if I understand this, what you are trying to tell me is, God and the universe see my paintings and my paintings become part of the universe, whether anyone else ever sees them or not."

God and the universe see all creation.

"But neither God nor the universe will pay my bills."

They will not. Neither God nor the universe gives a whit about bills. Bills go away. Everything goes away, except that which is created.

"OK, I don't think that makes any sense at all, but I guess it is something to think about." Lamb pondered and pondered some more. She paced and smoked two more cigarettes, lighting the second directly from the cherry of the first.

Hoof stood patiently in front of his black, 1964 Lincoln Continental. The engine had idled through a gallon of gas in the time Hoof and Lamb had been bargaining.

Finally, Lamb turned, faced Hoof, and looked him straight in the eyes. "You got a pen?"

Hold up the index finger of your writing hand.

Lamb held up the index finger of her right hand.

Hoof's pupils turned smoldering coal red.

Your signature is writ with fire.

THE A-1 TROPHY COMPANY
By Kelley Baker

"Who wants to eat dead fish?" Calvin bellows from the front office.

Karoly looks over at me and rolls his eyes. He's bending a piece of light green aluminum for his newest creation, a first place trophy to be given to one lucky team of seniors at the Powell Boulevard Convalescent Home's Annual Lawn Bowling tournament.

Calvin waddles in with a handful of gold plastic letters that say merely "74", the current year.

"Hey kid, before you start drilling those new bases throw these into some acetone and make them silver. Gold doesn't work for Karoly's latest work of art."

Being hung over, I'm not in a hurry to start drilling anyway. Not that inhaling acetone fumes will make me feel any better.

"So who wants dead fish?"

That's Calvin's way of asking if we want to go to lunch at the fish and chip place around the corner. Whenever we work

Saturdays Calvin buys lunch. Karoly only works Saturdays when we're behind schedule, which happens more often than not thanks to Calvin's over optimistic promises to the customers. I'm the only one who runs the drill press so I always work Saturdays since I'm still in high school and only work half days during the week.

Since the death of his wife, Calvin always works Saturdays. He doesn't have much of a home life now that Paul, his son, lives with his aunt and uncle.

Aunt Harriet and Uncle Bill never work Saturdays, which is fine. In addition to being brother and sister, Calvin and Harriet fight like cats and dogs. At least once a week, Aunt Harriet and Uncle Bill storm out of the office in the middle of the day.

Uncle Bill doesn't really storm out. Retired from the Air Force with a disability pension and a smashed voice box, he does everything slowly. He sits in a small back office engraving the tiny plaques we attach to the front of the trophies with double sticky tape and hope they don't fall off before they're handed out to the winners.

I like Uncle Bill even though it's hard to understand his raspy whisper.

Being the youngest, I do all the physical labor. Like unloading the heavy marble bases that get shipped to us whenever Calvin makes some shady deal. The delivery driver drops the ten, four hundred pound wooden crates on the sidewalk in front of the building. I crowbar them open, unpack the smaller boxes, and haul them down to the over crowded storage space in the basement using a busted up hand truck that's older than I am.

Uncle Bill always brings me water or a soda and accompanies me down the basement to Calvin's storage space. I label and stack the marble boxes as close to the front as possible because they're the only things that actually leave the storage space.

"What the hell is he keeping this for?" Uncle Bill rasps picking up a broken paper cutter.

I shake my head as he tosses it on to a pile of unopened Christmas ornament boxes from twenty years ago.

"All this useless junk. One day I should burn this whole place up." He whispers to me with a conspirators smile.

"How bout Kress?" Calvin says as I open a gallon can of acetone and pour it into an old coffee can.

"No Kress!" Karoly and I shout together.

The Kress Cafeteria is Calvin's go to spot and possibly the most depressing place on earth. Straight out of the nineteen fifties ancient hair-netted ladies in matching pink dresses, spoon out mushy canned vegetables along with bone dry turkey and gravy of a color not commonly found in nature. Plus, your choice of coffee or a glass of blueish milk that's been sitting on the counter for god-knows-how-long? All for a dollar ninety-nine.

At Kress Calvin is a rock star. All the old ladies know his balding head and loud Hawaiian shirts. They don't care that at sixty-four he's as tall as he is wide, cause he always flirts with them. All of them.

Calvin likes to say, "Eating at Kress is like Thanksgiving every day of the year."

I don't like Thanksgiving, even on Thanksgiving.

"Alright dead fish it is! How about we go in twenty minutes?" Calvin says as he waddles back up front.

Calvin doesn't drink coffee or coke but he always seems wired.

"And don't leave those numbers in the acetone too long, they'll get soft."

I don't respond because he tells me this every time. Karoly won't work with acetone. It's a very nasty chemical and there's no safety equipment, like a mask or rubber gloves. Breathing acetone fumes can't be any worse than smoking the Viceroys that Karoly loves.

As Calvin leaves Karoly looks over.

"Bart, you ever watch Addams Family on TV?"

I nod my head.

"Why watch? All work here!" Karoly shakes his head as he goes back to his metal bending.

That line is a recent variation on another of Karoly's favorites. Usually he says, "Hey Bart you go to zoo?" When I nod he replies, "Why go to zoo? All work here!"

Karoly and I share the back room. He designs and bends the various metals that make up the trophies we build. He's got a great eye for design and color. I'm not sure where this place would be without him.

Aunt Harriet says Karoly and his wife escaped from Hungary because of the communist regime. He's some sort of engineer, which is why he's able to design and create so many different kinds of trophies.

Aunt Harriet thinks he should be working for some big company but since his English isn't very good he's had a tough time finding higher paying work.

I try to imagine what it must have been like to escape from a communist country. Did they have to go through tunnels and climb walls with ropes? Did they have phony papers they had to show to soldiers at checkpoints?

I don't ask Karoly about this stuff and he never talks about himself. Mostly he talks about what he and his wife watch on

TV. I'm not sure what shows he's watching 'cause half the time I don't understand what he's saying.

The worst is when Aunt Harriet walks back to our room and tells Karoly to tell me the joke he told her earlier that he heard on TV. Karoly gets all happy and tells me some sort of joke and he and Aunt Harriet laugh. I never understand the jokes and they're not funny but I can always tell when he gets to the end 'cause he starts laughing.

For the rest of the day Karoly will look over at me and repeat the punch line and laugh. I laugh too 'cause I don't want to hurt his feelings.

Karoly always wears a white shirt and slacks to work and somehow manages to stay clean. I, on the other hand walk out of the place every evening with stains on my t-shirt and jeans and marble dust everywhere.

It only takes five minutes for the acetone to eat through the gold coating. I use an old toothbrush to make sure I get all the gold out of the tiny crevices. I go through a toothbrush every couple weeks as the brush parts fall out. I toss the now silver numbers in to the sink to soak in warm water to get the acetone off.

I asked Uncle Bill how come they don't make silver numbers and he said they do but Calvin's too cheap to buy 'em.

As jobs go, it's not a bad one. I go to school with Paul and Calvin is his dad. His adopted dad, but that's still a dad, even though Paul lives with Aunt Harriet and Uncle Bill now.

I don't know Paul all that well. He plays coronet in the marching band.

Paul has epilepsy. He starts shaking and gets this glazed look in his eyes and he's gone. It was eerie the first time I saw it up close. Calvin tells me to keep Paul away from the larger machines.

"Watch my kid, there's no market for a one armed trumpet player."

He'll go off on how Paul can't do this and can't do that. Sometimes he and Paul get physical, especially when Paul tries to use the drill press. They'll scuffle and Paul will throw Calvin to the ground.

Whenever they have a fight Calvin storms out swearing and Paul runs out the back door. Later I find Paul sound a sleep on the floor in the men's room in one of the stalls. I don't think he remembers their fights.

Once a month Calvin has me help him on Sunday morning. I go over to his apartment and load up my truck with junk that he sells at the flea market.

His cluttered apartment is on the first floor of a beautiful old building in a quiet neighborhood that's close enough to downtown so there's never any parking. I leave my truck in the middle of the street.

Calvin opens the window and passes boxes out to me from his living room. It's dark and all I can see are boxes everywhere.

As he hands me boxes he says things like, "Be careful with this one, it's worth more than you." or "Use both hands on this, it's breakable." "This one's full of cheap watches that I'm gonna make a killing on." "This one's full of snakes so put it up front with us." I know he doesn't have snakes in the box but if he wants it in the front seat why doesn't he just say so?

Once the truck is loaded with Calvin's useless crap he gives me his philosophy on life as we drive to the flea market.

"You know how I came up with the name of the company?"

I don't bother shaking my head or replying 'cause he's gonna tell me anyway.

"Most people don't know anything about trophies. They just know they need 'em. So what do they do? They look up trophies in the phone book and call the first name listed. So I look in the phone book myself. I see that Emerson's Trophies was way down on the list. I had to change the name of the business. But everyone in the business knows me and I can't just change my name so I asked myself what do I do? How do I move up and get more business? What would you do?"

I keep my eyes on the road.

"You would've gone out of business. You wouldn't know what to do. You see that's why I used the old brain." he taps a finger to his bald head.

"You know I never went to school. I was too smart. They couldn't teach me anything I didn't already know. Most people would take an ad out in the phone book. That's what they want you to do. So they can make more money off you and an ad doesn't help. I know that. I'm smarter than they are. So what would you do?"

He paused and I knew he was waiting for some response.

"I don't know…"

"Precisely! That's why you'd go out of business. But I'm smart. Smart like a fox. I knew what to do."

He pauses again. I don't know why and I really have nothing to say so I wait.

Finally he says, "So I called up the phone book people and tell them I've changed the name of my business. They say, oh yeah, what is it? And I say, A-1 Emerson's Trophies. See what I did there? I added the A-1. That puts my name number one in the phone book. And I don't have to change the name of the business because people still make out their checks to Emerson's Trophies. Pretty smart eh?"

While Calvin is congratulating himself on his superior business skills I quietly think to myself, "So when did A-1 American Trophies move in across the street and become first in the phone book?" But I don't ask.

His story stretches out long enough so that as he finishes I pull on to the gravel parking lot at the flea market. It hasn't officially opened its doors yet but there's already a line of cars and trucks waiting to unload.

"Okay kid you wait here and I'll go grab a cart so we can unload." He says as he slides off the front seat and out the door. At least he waited for me to stop this time.

In moments he's back and I'm unloading all of his precious cargo on to the cart under his watchful eye.

He slowly peels a twenty-dollar bill from a huge wad of cash he pulls out of his pocket. Before he hands it to me he always says, "Don't worry about picking me up, Uncle Bill is coming by later with Paul, they'll take me home."

He hands me the twenty.

"Plus you're too expensive, I'd go broke if I had to pay you to pick me up too. See you on Monday kid."

Before I can respond, Calvin pushes his cart full of junk off into the darkness and I go home and back to bed.

"Come on guys, dead fish time." Bellows Calvin as he walks in to the backroom. "Paul's hungry and I'm afraid he's gonna chew my arm off if I don't feed him soon."

Karoly continues bending a piece of orange colored aluminum.

"No lunch for me. I go home soon." He says.

"Come on Karoly I'm buyin'."

I look over at Karoly as he shakes his head. There's no way he's coming.

Calvin looks at me.

"Come on kid the three of us 'll go eat dead fish."

Karoly smiles as Calvin waddles out the door.

The Elephant & Castle is a British Pub just around the corner from the trophy shop.

Calvin is talking about something the whole way over. Between the traffic and the fact that I'm walking behind him, I can't hear a word he's saying. Paul just stares at his feet as he walks.

Inside the lights are dim and there's plenty of finished hard wood on the walls. What you can see of the walls anyway. There are framed pictures, street signs, and all sorts of other memorabilia to make you feel like you're somewhere in London.

We find a table near the door that already has menus laid out next to the silverware. It never takes much time to decide what to order cause it's either fish and chips or some kind of hideous looking beef pie. The big decision is do you want three or four pieces of over-cooked, deep fried, greasy cod?

As I pretend to study the menu the waitress comes to the table. She's wearing a white cotton t-shirt with faded jeans, her long auburn hair pulled back. I try not to stare. Maybe lunch with Calvin won't be so bad.

"Hi guys! I'm Janine; I'll be helping you today. Do you know what you'd like?"

"Yeah, you in pajamas!" Calvin says loudly.

Paul laughs and I want to crawl under the table.

I hate working Saturdays.

ABOUT THE WRITERS

Mark A. Nobles is a sixth generation Texan. Born on Fort Worth's infamous Jacksboro Highway, Mark proudly claims blood and kinship with Thunder Road's gamblers, outlaws, and wastrels. His work has appeared in or been published by Cowboy Jamboree, Sleeping Panther Review, Crimson Streets, Cleaver Magazine, Curating Alexandria, The Dead Mule School of Southern Literature, Gimmick Press, Haunted MTL, Road Kill Vol. 4, and other publications. He has produced and/or directed three feature documentaries and several short, experimental films. Mark lives in Fort Worth but hopes to die in the desert. He loves his two dogs, two daughters, and Texas, but not necessarily in that order. He can be found and followed on Facebook @ Flyin' Shoes Films.

Kelley Baker is the Angry Filmmaker. He's written and directed three fulllength features (*Birddog, The Gas Café, & Kicking Bird*), eight short films, and quite a few documentaries. His films have aired on PBS, Canadian and Australian television, and have been shown at Film Festivals including London, Sydney, Annecy, Sao Paulo, Sundance, and Edinburgh. In addition to his own films he was the sound designer on six of Gus Van Sant's feature films including, *My Own Private Idaho, Good Will*

Hunting and *Finding Forrester*. He's the author of *Road Dog*, and *The Angry Filmmaker Survival Guide: Part One & Part Two*. A Portland, Oregon native he spent seven years touring America in a used mini-van with a giant Chocolate Lab named Moses, showing his films at art house theaters, universities, and even biker bars. He is a sucker for rescue animals that seem to appear on his doorstep thanks to his daughter, Fiona. You'll find him hanging out at www.angryfilmmaker.com.